Lock Down Publications and Ca$h
Presents

I0658362

MONEY HUNGRY DEMONS 2

THE DEVILS YOU KNOW

A Novel By
TRANAY ADAMS

First Edition 2024

Printed in the United States of America

Lock Down Publications
P.O. Box 944
Stockbridge, GA 30281
www.lockdownpublications.com

Like our page on Facebook: Lock Down Publications
www.facebook.com/lockdownpublications.ldp

Stay Connected with Us!

Text **LOCKDOWN** to 22828 to stay up-to-date with new releases, sneak peaks, contests and more…

Like our page on Facebook:
Lock Down Publications

Join Lock Down Publications/The New Era Reading Group

Visit our website:
www.lockdownpublications.com

Follow us on Instagram:
Lock Down Publications

Email Us: We want to hear from you!

Chapter 1

Shirvetta, Biggie and Baby Girl were sitting in the living room, watching *Power,* when someone knocked at the door. They were so engrossed in the cable television show that no one wanted to answer the door.

"Get that, sis." Biggie nudged Baby Girl.

"Nah. It's your turn. I got it when the pizza came," Baby Girl replied, opening up the Dominoes box and taking another slice.

Biggie looked at Shirvetta, who was snuggled under a blanket on the opposite couch. "Boy, please, you're the man of the house, since your father isn't here, so you needa answer it."

Biggie took a breath, grabbed his gun off the coffee table and walked to the front door. He stole a peek through the peep-hole and saw his second oldest sibling standing on the other side.

"Who is it, Biggie?" Shirvetta asked.

"Golden," Biggie replied, unlocking the door and pulling it open. Golden stepped inside the house, pulling off his hood and looking over the living room. Biggie closed and locked the door behind him. He looked Golden over with a frown, taking in his all black attire.

"'Sup witchu, bro? You dressed up like you're about to put in some work," Biggie said.

4

"That's what I was about to say?" Baby Girl chimed in. She tossed what was left of her pizza into the box and smacked the crumbs off her hands.

"You look like somethin' is botherin' you. What's the matter, son?" Shirvetta asked with concern, throwing the blanket aside and rising from the sofa. She could tell by the scowl on Golden's face something was troubling him.

"Niggaz set me and Aries's crib on fire and shot it up," Golden replied.

"Oh my God, are you okay, baby?" Shirvetta approached, checking him for wounds. Baby Girl came from the opposite side of him, examining him for wounds also.

"I'm good, ma. Really," Golden assured Shirvetta, kissing her forehead. He turned to Baby Girl and kissed her on the cheek.

"Bro, you know how we roll. All you gotta do is point 'em out, and I'll make 'em a memory," Biggie told him. He didn't have a problem taking someone's life, and this situation gave him the perfect excuse.

"Honestly, I don't know," Golden admitted. "But listen, I'm not here for that. I'm here on the account of Cowboy. Rich Loc had some fools kidnap 'em and I think he plans on killin' 'em. We've gotta bust a move tonight."

Biggie scowled and waved him off. "Man, forget that nigga. He's on his own."

"What chu mean he's on his own? That's our big brother. He's blood," Golden countered.

"That nigga ceased being my brother after he put hands on Baby Girl, beat cho ass, and then threw ma across the room, like a rag doll," Biggie shot back. "If whoever has 'em decides to kill 'em, they'll be doin' me a favor, 'cause I fa sho' planned on doin' it myself."

"I can't believe this," Golden replied heatedly. "They got bruh over some mess we all participated in and you wanna leave 'em to be crucified? Son, I don't care what we go through internally, we're family. We can settle our differences later. But when outsiders start messin' with our own, they get dealt with, A-sap. Ya dig, baby brother?"

"Yeah. I dig. I'm still not budgin' though. I'm standin' on what I said, 'fuck Cowboy'," Biggie said.

***

This was the first time Biggie had cussed in front of their mother, so Golden knew he was dead ass. There wasn't any way he could get him to change his mind, so he thought he'd try to persuade the women.

"Baby Girl, I know you got cho big brother back," Golden said, locking eyes with his sister.

Baby Girl went to step forward, but Biggie stepped in front of her, blocking her path. He shook his head, no. Baby Girl looked at Golden from over Biggie's shoulder with sorrowful eyes. She wasn't sure of what she should do. She wanted to roll out with Golden and get Cowboy back, but then again, she also wanted to stay on her twin's good side. They had a unique bond, seeing as how they were fraternal and came out of the same womb on the same day. Baby Girl dropped her head and fidgeted with her fingers.

"Ma, you gon' leave yo' son hangin'? Regardless of what Cowboy did, he's still one of your boys," Golden told Shirvetta, taking note of the hand impression on her neck from Cowboy choking her.

"Drop it, Golden. The nigga said it himself that mom's is not his real old lady. So, what does she look like ridin' out witchu to put the smash on whomever has that nigga?" Biggie interjected, pulling his mother behind him. She looked like she wanted to go with Golden, but there was something within her mind holding her back.

"My nigga, last time I checked, Shirvetta Love was a grown ass woman, who can speak for herself. Ma," Golden looked at his mother, hoping she'd come along on his rescue mission.

"Tell 'em you not goin' nowhere, ma. Tell 'em you refuse to bust yo' gun behind yo' illegitimate ass son, who put his hands on you. And don't chu feel bad about it either, 'cause that demon doesn't deserve a mother's love. As a matter of fact, son doesn't deserve anyone's love." Biggie's face was scrunched and a vein on his forehead was pronounced.

"Golden, I—" Shirvetta began, but she was cut off by Golden throwing up his hand.

"Spare me the excuses, ma, I don't need 'em," Golden said with teary eyes. "Y'all don't want to come with me to get Cowboy back? Cool. I'll do it my damn self, but if I get murdered in the process, just know it will be all y'all's fault." He motioned a finger around to all of them. "If you can live with that, then you never cared about me in the first place." Golden turned around, wiping the tears from his eyes, as he walked towards the front door.

"Bruh, you can't put that on us. Come on now. That ain't right, yo." Biggie said, starting to feel guilty.

Golden walked out of the house, leaving the front door wide open. He hopped over the gated fence with one hand and sped walked toward his whip.

"I'm not letting my baby go off alone. If something happens to 'em, I'll be sick," Shirvetta told Biggie, holding his chubby face in her hands. "Baby Girl, catch up with Golden and tell 'em we're comin' along. I'll be getting the armor and guns." She darted to the back of the house, where the armory was located.

Baby Girl went to chase after Golden, but Biggie grabbed her arm. She looked back at him like he'd called her out of her name.

"Stay outta that shit. Remember that nigga put his hands on you," Biggie said with a mad dog expression.

Baby Girl snatched her arm back and looked at him, angrily. "People make mistakes, Biggie. No one is perfect. Like Golden said, Cowboy's our brother. If someone's gonna hurt 'em, then they're gonna have to see all of us behind that."

Baby Girl ran out of the house as fast as she could, calling after Golden, hoping to catch up with him.

"Golden, wait, wait. We're coming with you."

Urrrrk!

Golden busted a U-turn in the middle of the street, speeding past Baby Girl, without looking her way.

A second later, Shirvetta ran out of the house wearing a bulletproof-vest over her wife beater. She ran out into the middle of the residential street, looking down the block at the back lights of Golden's vehicle.

"Golden. Golllldennn," Shirvetta called after him until the rear lights of his car disappeared. Baby Girl ran out of the yard and stood beside her. Shirvetta wrapped her arms around her, and they continued to stare down the block, where Golden's whip vanished.

"Ma, I hope he'll be okay," Baby Girl said with glassy eyes.

"Me too, baby. Me too," Shirvetta replied, taking an exasperated breath.

Biggie stood in the doorway, watching the entire scene unfold. He lingered there a moment longer, before walking back in the house.

***

Aries stared out of the passenger window as she waited for Golden. Her heart was beating fast and her palms were clammy. She was nervous about the possibilities that night. Golden was expecting her to kick down the door of wherever Cowboy was being held with guns blazing. But she was terrified Rich Loc would wind up getting killed in the process. She loved Rich Loc, just as much as she loved Golden, and she'd die knowing she was involved with his being murdered. She didn't know how she was going to do it, but she had to lure Rich Loc from the spot before her and the Loves hit the place.

Come on, bitch! Think, think, think, Aries thought. She looked at the driver's door when she saw Golden's reflection in the passenger window. He slid in behind the wheel and slammed the door shut. Aries's forehead wrinkled seeing him frowning and glassy-eyed. She'd expected him to return with his family for their mission, but he'd come back alone. She knew then that something had gone down.

"G, what happened in there?" Aries asked.

"What happened is, my muthafuckin' family is leaving my brother for dead. I can't believe this shit." Golden slammed his fist on the dashboard in a fit of anger. He cranked up his whip, pulled away from the curb and busted a U-turn in the middle of the street. Aries looked through the driver's window, to see Baby Girl running out of the house, calling his name.

"Babe, your sister's calling after you. Maybe they changed their minds about coming along," Aries told him.

Golden kept his attention focused on the road ahead. "Fuck them. It's too late now. It's just you and me, ma. You got my back, right?" Golden glanced at her.

"You know I got chu, 'til the very end," Aries assured him, interlocking her fingers with his and kissing his hand. He grinned and kissed her hand back.

A'ight, big bruh, hang tight, the cavalry is on the way, Golden thought, zipping up the street and leaving debris in his wake.

Chapter 2

Heavy's eyes popped open as he gasped for air. His face was covered in sweat bubbles and fear was prevalent in his eyes. He took his contraband cellphone from its hiding place and slid off his bunk. His new cellie sat up on his bunk, frowning and rubbing his eye. He'd heard Heavy making noise in his sleep and figured he'd had a nightmare. They'd gotten rather close during his short time there, so he was concerned with his well-being.

"Yo, main man, what's the deal?" Quentin asked groggily.

"Calling home, bruh. I just hadda nightmare I hope doesn't come true," Heavy replied, holding his cellular to his ear and pacing the floor. "Come on, Goddess, pick up," he said under his breath, referring to Shirvetta.

"I'm not tryna be all up in yours, main man, but what was ya nightmare about?" Quentin yawned, stretching his arms and legs.

"One of my kids, man," Heavy replied, disconnecting the call and hitting Shirvetta again.

"What about one of your kids?"

"One of them was killed in my nightmare, and that shit felt so real."

"Hopefully it's not," Quentin said, jumping down to the floor and saying a quick prayer for his cellmate's children. He then climbed back up to his bunk.

"Hello? Thank God you answered," Heavy sighed with relief, hearing Shirvetta's voice.

"Why? What's goin' on?" Shirvetta asked, worried.

"Nothing. I just had a fucked up dream that one of the kids had gotten killed," Heavy replied. "Is everyone good?"

"Uh, yeah, everyone is fine, baby," Shirvetta said. She sounded unsure and Heavy picked up on it.

"Nuh unh. Don't lie to me," Heavy told her, angrily. "If somethin' has happened to one of my babies, then I wanna know. And I wanna know right now, Shirvetta."

Shirvetta gave Heavy the rundown on what happened between the family and Golden. He was pissed, and she couldn't blame him.

"Shirvetta Michelle Love," a scowling Heavy continued, pacing the floor. "If anythang happens to our boys, I swear on my life, I'm gonna bring down fire and brimstone on yo' fuckin' a—"

Shirvetta hung up on him, cutting him short. He looked at his cellphone like it was a part of an alien spacecraft. "I know her ass didn't hang up on me." He tried calling her back, but her cellphone went directly to voicemail. So, he verbally assaulted her in his voice message. He tried calling Golden a few times, but he didn't answer.

"Is everything copacetic?" Quentin asked, concerned.

"Nah, my nig, everythang is far from copacetic," Heavy replied, from his bunk. He was lying on his back and clutching his cellphone against his stomach.

"What's the matter with yo' pups, man?"

Heavy usually kept his personal business to himself, but it was something inside him that was dying to vent. He gave his cellmate the four-one-one on the situation with his boys, and then sighed heavily. It felt like a boulder had been lifted from his back, after telling homie what was going on and how he was hot about it.

11

"Damn, G. I'm sorry to hear that," Quentin shook his head and laid back on his bunk. "But if your second oldest son, Golden, is as smart and dangerous as you say he is, then I'm sure the young nigga can get your oldest boy back."

"I sincerely hope so, bruh. I really do," Heavy said, staring up at the bottom of his cellmate's bunk. He was so worried about Golden and Cowboy. He knew he wouldn't get any sleep that night, until he was sure they were good. So, he vowed to blow up Golden's cell until he got an answer.

***

Cowboy had urinated and defecated on himself, after Rich Loc tased him so many times. His heart was beating funny, and he experienced occasional tremors. Still, he didn't fold under the intense scrutiny and unbearable pain.

"You're one bad muthafucka, son. You know that? My locs and I have never hadda work this hard to get a vic to crack. You should consider this an honor, me having to use my girls and all. Yep. It's been a long time since me and the ladies have been out on a date." Rich Loc sat a length of velvet the size of a small rug on an end table. He drew its string and rolled it open. He feasted his eyes on a set of unique knives with diamond dust edges and spiked knuckle guards. Each blade had its own name engraved on it in Arabic. A devilish smile graced Rich Loc's lips, when he saw his reflection in the weapons of torture.

Cowboy watched as Rich Loc removed all of his jewelry and set it aside on the end table. He pulled his shirt over his head and tossed it aside. He removed a blue bandana from his left back pocket and tied it around the lower half of his face. Next, he put on a pair of black latex gloves and picked up the biggest knife in his collection. Staring at his reflection in the blade, Rich Loc fixed his hair and checked his teeth for any food that may be stuck between them.

"You come anywhere near me with that knife, and I'ma bend you over and fuck you with it," Cowboy swore.

"My dogs are hungry, real hungry, so each time you refuse to tell me what I wanna know, I'm gonna slice off a part of you and feed it to 'em," Rich Loc told him. "I think I'll start with your left ear. Yeah. The left ear will be juuuust perfect," he licked his top row of teeth as he walked towards Cowboy, to make good on his threat. The hounds his hitters held on leashes licked their chops in anticipation of being fed parts of Cowboy.

Cowboy grunted as he rocked back and forth in the chair, trying desperately to get free.

***

"Look, Rich, uh, I mean, Golden. I'm sorry. I didn't mean to call you by his name," Aries apologized, cussing herself out in her head. *You stupid ass bitch. It will be yo' fault if he doesn't go along with your plan now.*

Golden frowned at her and gripped the steering wheel tight. He gritted and fought back his ill feelings. His mind was on getting Cowboy back in one piece.

"What I'm tryna say is, Jesus Christ, I know you don't wanna hear this shit." She took a breath and shook her head. She was so terrified of telling him what she felt he needed to know, that her hands were shaking.

"You already opened Pandora's Box, so you may as well speak yo' peace."

"Okay. I've been fuckin' with dude for a lil over a year now. In that time, I believe, if a person is cool and treats you decently, that you can start to grow feelings for them, even if you're not supposed to."

Golden nodded.

"What I'm saying is, I know you wanna rock dude to sleep so this entire thing won't come back to bite us in the ass, but I need time to make peace with it. You understand?"

Golden nodded. "I understand where you're coming from, so now what do you suggest we do?"

Aries didn't respond, but when Golden looked at her, he could tell that she was thinking about something. Once she was ready to speak her mind, she cleared her throat.

"Okay. I got a way we can rescue your brother, without anyone getting killed."

"How are we gonna do that?"

"We can stage me getting robbed," Aries replied. "I'll call dude and tell 'em what's up, on my way to the hospital. Then he'll come running, leaving yo' brother alone with his goons. That's when you swing into action, lay them niggaz down, and save yo' brother."

"You think this nigga is gonna buy you getting robbed?"

"With the way I plan to play it? Yes."

"So what do you plan to do?"

"You recall when you told me yo' father had you guys studying human anatomy before y'all jumped into the jack game?" Golden parked inside the parking lot of a supermarket and turned off the ignition. "I figure I'll have you stab me in some place where I won't bleed to death, to make shit look realistic. I know dude will buy it then."

Golden started at Aries for a minute. He noticed during their conversation that she didn't call Rich Loc by his name. He didn't have to ask her why, because he already knew she was trying to disassociate herself from him, so she wouldn't be in her feelings once he finally blew his ass away.

Golden leaned back against the headrest, taking a deep breath. "I can't believe the shit I let chu talk me into, yo."

Aries' heart was beating fast as she waited for Golden's response. He couldn't see it, but her fingers were crossed on the side of her leg.

"A'ight. Fuck it," Golden said, starting up his ride. Aries grinned and thanked God for his cooperation. "The surveillance cameras behind this supermarket don't work. We can do what we needa do right here."

Golden parked behind the supermarket and removed a bowie knife from the armrest. He hopped out, drawing the blade from its sheath, with Aries following behind him. He faced her, while she stood with her back against the building. She held up her shirt and Golden felt around the right side of her body. He knew her most vital organs were on her left, and he could kill her if he struck her there. Golden located the perfect spot to poke Aries. He took a breath and looked up at her. His face was one of anger and regret. Holding his gaze, she felt everything that he had at that moment. That wasn't going to stop her from going through with her plan, though.

"A'ight, brace yo'self," Golden told her. He focused his sight on the precise area he planned to penetrate. Then, without warning, he jabbed her swiftly. She howled, like a wounded dog, and dropped to her knees. She held her bleeding wound and looked at her dripping hand.

"Sssssss, gotdamn, that shit hurts. Fuck. Mmmmm," Aries frowned and clenched her jaws. "Okay. Okay. We gotta make this look good, so I want chu, I want chu to kick me in the face."

"What?" Golden scowled, looking at her with disbelief. He'd heard what she said. He just couldn't believe she'd said it.

"This will be the cherry on top, bae. Remember, we're tryna make this look good."

Golden stared down at Aries, balling his fists and clenching his jaws tighter. He was angry and hurt that she'd go through all of this shit, just to keep that nigga Rich Loc alive. Before he knew it, he'd kicked her in the face, and she dropped flat on her stomach. She lay groaning in pain, with her eyes rolled to the back of her head.

Golden teared up as he towered over Aries. The thought of her going through this much suffering over a nigga that wasn't him shattered his heart into a thousand pieces. He blinked back the tears that so desperately wanted to coat his cheeks and cleared his throat, before speaking again.

"Aye, aye," Golden shook Aries repeatedly. She looked up at him lazily and tried to get up twice, before she was eventually able to sit up. She pulled out her cellular and leaned up against the wall.

"How do I look?" Aries asked, turning her face from left to right so he could get a good look at his handiwork.

"Fucked up," Golden replied, examining her injury.

"Perfect," Aries said, about to dial emergency.

Golden grabbed the hand that held her cellphone. "Hold up. Gemme ten minutes to clear the area before you hit Jake."

"A'ight."

Golden had walked halfway to his car when Aries called him back. He stopped and looked over his shoulder at her.

"I love you."

Golden looked at the ground for a moment. He was confused and conflicted about how to respond to her, since he felt she'd been playing with his emotions. He knew he was just in his feelings and still loved her though.

"I love you, too, shorty," Golden said, hopping into his car and backing up. Aries watched him turn around and race out of the supermarket's parking lot.

Chapter 3

Golden sat parked on the opposite side of the school, with a watchful eye on its entrance. He stole a glance at his timepiece, noting he'd hung up with Aries a few minutes ago. He looked at his cellphone as it vibrated in his lap and saw it was his pops. Heavy had been calling him back to back, but he kept ignoring his calls. He was on demon time now, so everything else had to wait.

Golden slid his cellphone inside his pocket. He looked up at the school and saw Rich Loc running out, like he'd just robbed a bank. The millionaire dope-boy unlocked the back gate of the school's parking lot, drove out, and then locked the gate before whisking away. The engine of his ride growled ferociously as he sped up the block, ignoring stop sign after stop sign. The moment he was gone, Golden tied a black bandana over the lower half of his face and grabbed his twin pistols with the silencers. He hopped out his whip, jogging across the street with his head on a swivel. He blew the lock off the back gate, kicked it open, and stormed the facility's grounds. He opened the back exit door of the main building, carefully closing it behind him, and creeping inside.

Golden could hear fists pounding against flesh and the pain-filled grunts of a man. He knew, without a doubt, it was his brother on the wrong side of that beating. The thought of mothafuckas lying hands on his sibling infuriated him. He scowled and gripped his sticks tighter. He pressed his back against the wall and eased alongside it until he reached the door that led to the boy's locker room. Hunched over, Golden snuck through a maze of lockers, with the beating growing louder and louder as he neared the shower room.

Golden took a peek around the corner of the entrance of the shower room. Three locs holding the leashes of Rottweilers and assault rifles were crowded around Cowboy. They looked on as a fourth loc gave him crucial face and body shots. Cowboy's blood flew in every direction, splattering on the floor. The Rottweilers licked it right up.

I'ma getchu outta this, bro, you just sit tight, Golden thought, pulling his head back around the corner. He stared down at the ground as he considered his next move.

The scent of an unrecognized human drew one of the dogs' attention to the entrance of the shower room. The hound started barking and the others followed suit. The locs holding the leashes to the Rottweilers, looked to the entrance. Unbeknownst to Golden, they saw one of his sneakers peeking out from where he was hiding behind the wall. One of the locs tapped the one that was giving Cowboy a beating. He stopped pounding on Cowboy and turned around to the entrance of the shower room. The loc that had tapped him pointed at Golden's sneaker from where he was hiding. While the hounds were barking, the loc that was punishing Cowboy, grabbed his assault rifle from where he'd propped it against the wall. Cocking it quickly, he gripped it with both hands and whispered into the ear of one of his comrades. His words spread like the ass cheeks of a stripper, performing on the stage at DOA.

On the count of three, the locs released their Rottweilers from their chain-linked leashes and they took off in Golden's direction. They bent the corner growling and barking harshly.

"Aaaaah," Golden hollered as he was viciously attacked by the bloodthirsty hounds.

Suddenly, there was silence. The locs looked at one another with confusion in their eyes. The loc that was beating on Cowboy, called for the dogs to come back, but they didn't return. He signaled for the rest of the locs to follow him, as he took a step toward the entrance of the shower room. The locs discarded their leashes. As quietly as they possibly could, they crept towards the entrance, assault rifles at the ready. They had taken a mere three steps when they saw blood pouring across the floor of the shower room's entrance.

The loc at the forefront frowned and gave his comrades the signal to stop. He pointed at the blood at the entrance of the shower room. A satanic smile spread across his lips, as well as those of the other locs.

"Whoever that was, we got his bitch ass, cuz." the loc at the forefront announced.

"Hold up. Where the fuck are the d—" One of the locs was cut short when Golden, both guns extended in front of him, rolled past the shower room's entrance. He squeezed the triggers of his Glizzies back to back, lying down all of the locs except for one, before disappearing on the other side of the shower room's entrance.

"Arrrrrr," the surviving loc clenched his teeth, fighting back the pain of the gunshot wound in his thigh. He was posted up against the wall of the shower room, with his assault rifle held up against his chest. He tore off the lower half of his shirt and tied it tight around his thigh, to slow the blood flow. He could have sworn he saw Cowboy moving, so he pointed his assault rifle at him. To his surprise, he was still strapped to the chair with his head bowed.

"I don't know who you are, or what cho beef is, but chu fucked up, cuz. You fucked up, big time," the surviving loc called out from where he was hidden against the shower room wall. He was about to say something else, but a thought crossed his mind. His forehead crinkled and he looked at Cowboy. That's when he gathered that whoever it was that launched the attack was there to rescue him.

The surviving loc grinned evilly, sucked his teeth, and limped over to Cowboy. Standing beside him, he used his assault rifle to lift his chin from his chest. Cowboy, eyes narrowed, face lumpy and bleeding, groaned painfully.

"Oh, so this is what chu are here for, huh, cuz? You stuck yo' neck out for this fuckin' tweaker? Huh?" the surviving loc, who was looking at the shower room's entrance, called out to Golden. He recalled the track marks on the inside of Cowboy's arm, after Rich Loc had him and the homies beat him and strip him down to his birthday suit.

"Tweaker or not, that's my family, and I'm not leavin' this bitch without 'em," Golden called out from where he was hidden. He was glad old boy was feeling chatty because it gave him time to figure out his next move.

"Check this out, bro. I got Yolanda to this nigga's cap right now, you got 'til the count of three to pitch yo' gun and step out from wherever you are witcho hands up. One, two—" The last number died on the tip of the surviving locs' tongue, as a golden twinkle caught the corner of his eye. When he looked, he saw the unique golden knives Rich Loc had laid out to filet Cowboy. Seeing all the blades were there, except for two, made his brows furrow.

Chapter 4

Before the surviving loc could make his next move, Cowboy had already sprang into action. He whacked the assault rifle out of his face as it fired. He leaped from the chair with a unique golden knife in each hand. With a grunt, he slammed a blade down to its hilt on each side of the loc's skull. Blood squirted from the head wounds and poured below the knives' fist-guards. The loc's eyes fluttered and blood spilled out of them. He crashed to the floor, twitching.

Furious, Cowboy scanned the ground for the loc's assault rifle, until he located it. Picking it up, he checked the weapon's clip, smacked it back into its belly and cocked it. He stood over the loc with the golden knives in his skull, spraying his ass until the assault rifle clicked empty. Next, he took the assault rifle by its barrel, using it like a fire ax, he bludgeoned his victim's face until it caved in. Breathing heavily, Cowboy dropped to his knees and tossed the assault rifle aside. He looked up at the ceiling and roared like a tiger. Seeing someone approaching from the corner of his eye, he dove to the floor, rolling and coming back up with the assault rifle. He and Golden drew down on each other at the same time. The shower room was quiet save for Cowboy's labored breathing.

"Big bruh, relax. It's me. Golden." Golden told him. He kept his sticks on him a moment longer, before tucking them back in his waistband. He threw up his hands, to prove to Cowboy he wasn't a threat.

21

A second later, Cowboy lowered the assault rifle and used it as a crutch to push back up on his feet. He was so weak he buckled under his weight. He went to take a step forward and buckled again. Golden rushed over to give him some support. He tried to take the assault rifle from him, but he held fast.

Golden took stock of Cowboy's wounds and shook his head. Rich Loc and those old buster ass flunkies of his had done a real number on him. Scowling, Golden looked over the corpses of the locs he and his brother had laid down. He wished he had the power to bring their asses back to life just so he could kill them again, for what they had done to his brother.

"Lemme help you put on yo' clothes, G," Golden helped Cowboy sit down in the chair he was strapped in. He helped him slip on his clothes, put on his sneakers, and then draped his jacket over his shoulders. He couldn't help feeling like a parent assisting their toddler with getting dressed.

"Come on, bro, let's raise up outta here." Golden grasped Cowboy's hand and pulled him back to his feet. Cowboy growled under his breath from the soreness of his wounds. Golden threw his arm around his shoulders, and they walked out of the shower room.

***

"You the only fam that soldiered up and came to get me?" Cowboy asked through busted lips, sneaking a look through the side-view mirror. He thought he'd seen a car or two tailing them for backup, but there wasn't a vehicle in sight.

Keeping his focus on the road, Golden gave his brother a nod. Instantly, Cowboy's heart sank to his stomach and his eyes watered. He stared out of the passenger window and swallowed the lump of hurt in his throat. It crushed him to know that the rest of his family didn't give a fuck about him. As much shit as he popped at them, if any of them needed his help, he would have ridden out, no questions asked. It was fuck them now. They didn't care about him, so he, in return, didn't care about them.

Fuck 'em! I don't need 'em, Cowboy thought, as a lone tear crept out the corner of his eye. Sniffling, he wiped it away with his thumb.

Golden saw Cowboy's sorrowful eyes through his reflection in the passenger window. He grasped his shoulder in an attempt to comfort him, but he shrugged him off.

"I'm good," Cowboy told him, taking in his surroundings. He noticed they were jumping on the highway. His brows wrinkled, wondering where they were headed. "Fuck we goin'?"

"One of my spots in C.T.," Golden reported.

"I'ma needa lil something-something to get my mind right," Cowboy replied.

Golden nodded in response, knowing exactly what his brother needed, dope.

***

"Grrrrrrrrraaaaah," Cowboy hollered and clenched his jaws. He squeezed Golden's hand like a pregnant woman in labor. He'd just settled down inside an alcohol bath. The warm water bubbled and slowly turned orange from his wounds.

"You got this shit, bro. You got this!" Golden assured him with glassy eyes. Seeing his brother in so much pain hurt his heart. He was going to be on that nigga Rich Loc's head now.

On my momma, that ho-ass nigga not gettin' no more passes. I don't give a fuck about what cap shorty throws at me.

Suddenly, Cowboy smacked his other hand on Golden's and squeezed it. He clenched his jaws tighter, fighting back the pain that nearly covered his entire body. Tears burst out of Cowboy's pink eyes and poured down his cheeks. He felt like someone had drenched him in gasoline and lit him on fire.

"I'm gonna kill 'em, you hear me, Golden? I'm gonna kill everyone who has ever caused me pain. I don't give a fuck who they are," Cowboy swore, snot peaking out of his nose. "Momma, brother, sister. Any and everybody gon get it."

Golden didn't have a clue that Cowboy meant his words literally. Without a doubt, he was going to give all of those who harmed him halos.

"Nah. We're gon' get 'em, bro. You and me, ya feel me?" Golden replied, wiping away his tears.

Golden washed Cowboy up, cleaned and bandaged his wounds, and assisted him with putting on his underwear. Golden chopped it up with Cowboy, while staring out of the bedroom window. Cowboy was preparing a syringe of dope and he didn't want to see him shooting that shit.

Cowboy's body was racked with pain but things changed once the heroin invaded his system. He felt like he was lying on a bed of fluffy clouds with the warm sun shining on him, and an array of colorful flowers blooming around him. He laughed as he watched fat, white babies fly around him, sucking pacifiers and playing musical instruments.

After a while, Golden turned to Cowboy and found him wearing a strange look on his face. Golden's face balled up with animosity and he clenched his fists. He couldn't wait until he got his hands on that bitch-ass nigga, Rich Loc. His ho-ass was going to regret the day he ever laid hands on his brother.

Chapter 5

Rich Loc stood in the hospital's elevator lobby, punching the up button and tapping his foot impatiently. He began pacing the floor and glancing at the numbers above the elevator doors every five seconds. He glanced at his Roley and shook his head like it didn't make any goddamn sense how long the elevator was taking.

"Fuck this shit," Rich Loc cussed under his breath. It was killing him to know exactly what happened to Aries and if she was okay or not. With those thoughts on his mind, he fled the lobby and headed to the staircase. He went up the stairs four steps at a time in his Timbs, never stopping to catch his breath. Rich Loc burst through the door of the eleventh-floor panting and sweating, like he had the Devil chasing after him.

Rich Loc walked briskly down the hallway, pulling his blue bandana from his left back pocket and wiping his sweaty face. He marched right over to the nurses' station and requested Aries' room number, which he'd forgotten on the drive over.

"I'm sorry, sir, we don't have anyone here by Gabriella Milton," the short, portly Asian nurse told him.

Rich Loc frowned. "You sure? She's dark skinned, probably about five-foot-four, very curvaceous, bubble butt."

The Asian nurse's forehead wrinkled as she stared out the corners of her eyes, thinking. Her eyes lit up as she recalled someone he may be talking about. "Oh, you mean Aries Wilkerson, try room 308. It's down the hall, to your left," She told him, then answered the telephone.

Rich Loc wore a dumbfounded look on his face as he stood at the nurses station. He couldn't understand why his lady was checked in at the hospital under another name.

The Asian nurse hung up after taking a call. She was surprised to find Rich Loc still standing at her desk. "I'm sorry, sir, is there anything else you'd like for me to help you with?"

Rich Loc didn't reply. It was like he'd been hypnotized.

"Sir? Sir? Hello." she waved her hand before his eyes.

"Huh?" Rich Loc said, snapping out of it.

"Is there something else you'd like me to help you with?"

"Uhhh, nah. I'm good. Thanks anyway," Rich Loc told her. He then speed walked down the hallway, with his neck on a crane, looking for Aries' room.

As soon as Rich Loc spotted the room number, he rushed through the door and found Aries lying up in bed. She was dressed in one of those blue hospital gowns and an IV was in her arm. She looked really tired, but when she saw Rich Loc, she perked up and greeted him with a big smile. Rich Loc smiled back and rushed over to her bedside, pulling up a chair and taking her hand into his. He kissed her on the forehead and the lips. He then sat down and kissed her hand, staring into her eyes lovingly. She stared back at him with the same look in her eyes. She would never get over how she managed to get two of the biggest gangstas in New York to fall for her.

"Baby, tell me what happened? Who stabbed you?" Rich Loc asked, looking greatly concerned.

"I don't know his name, but he was Japanese, maybe Chinese," Aries told him. "He was definitely affiliated. Anyway, he ran up on me with a knife, and demanded my purse. I said no. That's when he stabbed me, and when I fell, he kicked me in the face. By the time I came around, I saw him running off with my purse."

Rich Loc's face had contorted into a mask of hatred, while listening to his lover recount what happened to her. "Gemme a description, baby. I'ma find this nigga for you and make 'em pay for his transgressions. On Crip."

"Richard, please, I'd rather just put this behind me and move forward," Aries said with a sorrowful look in her eyes.

"Nah," Rich Loc shook his head. "Fuck that. No one gets away with putting hands on my queen and walks away unscathed. Now, tell me what this Buddha Head looks like."

Aries exhaled, like what he asked had taken a lot out of her, but she was actually playing her role, and giving herself enough time to think. "Okay. He looked young, really young. He was kinda muscular, too. Oh, and blasted."

"Blasted?" Rich Loc frowned, looking clueless.

"Yeah. You know, hella tattoos," Aries replied. "He also had hazel eyes, blonde box braids, and a scar on his chin." She described the most bizarre-looking Chinese man she could think of, knowing he'd never find him in a million years, no matter how hard he tried, and that was the point.

"I'll find 'em, you hear me? Even if I gotta turn this city upside down and shake it 'til his ass falls out, I'll get 'em," Rich Loc swore, kissing her hand again.

Aries's brows furrowed as something on the television caught her eyes. Rich Loc noticed the expression on her face and looked at the T.V. He thought his mind was playing tricks on him when he saw what was on the screen.

"Turn this up, babe." Rich Loc told Aries, without turning away from the television. Aries obliged him and sat the remote beside her.

A female anchor stood with the same school Cowboy was held hostage in, in the background.

"A total of five men and four Rottweilers were found dead inside the boys' shower room, here at Marcus Garvey High School. It is not clear what happened, but police are leaning towards it being a drug deal gone bad…"

"Oh, shit, shit, shit." Rich Loc hopped up from his chair and ran to the door. He closed and locked it.

"Bae, what's the matter?" Aries sat up in bed. She played the role of concerned girlfriend wonderfully.

"That's the same school where we took that bitch ass nigga that stole my work, to torture him," Rich Loc told her, picking up the hospital's telephone. "All of those bodies gotta be some of my locs, but I needa know if dude is among the lot that was hit." He dialed the number he had in mind, but he couldn't get through the line. "Yo, how do you dial out this joint?"

"Press pound, three and then dial the number," Aries told him. "Who're you calling?"

"I've got a detective on my payroll. He may know something about this." Rich Loc listened as the phone rang. When his inside man answered, he began firing off questions. "Yeah. I'm watching the shit right now," he glanced over his shoulder at the news report. "A'ight. I don't care what time it is, call me back. I'm not gonna be able to sleep 'til I know what's up." He disconnected the call and plopped back down in the chair beside Aries' bed. He wore a mad dog stare as he continued to watch the report, and Aries rubbed his head affectionately.

Rich Loc nearly broke his neck, rushing to answer the telephone when his inside man called back. Aries looked at him in anticipation, as he chopped it up with his guy. The moment Rich Loc closed his eyes and bit his bottom lip, she knew he'd gotten some bad news.

"A'ight, Rollins, good looking out" Rich Loc disconnected the call and hung up the telephone. He dropped to his knees at Aries' bedside, and buried his face into the mattress, screaming his head off. She rubbed his head again, as he released all of his frustrations.

"What did he say, Rich?" Aries asked.

"He gave me the names of every nigga they rolled up outta that school," Rich Loc reported, getting off his knees. "I was familiar with all of 'em, so you know what that means. Ya boy got away."

"Damn. I'm sorry, boo."

"It's all good 'cause I'ma catch up with homie. Just like I'ma catch up with the chink that robbed my lady," Rich Loc assured her. "My word is bond." He pulled out a big ass knot of money and unfolded it. "How much that nigga hit chu for, ma?"

"Don't worry about it, baby. I'm okay."

"That's not the point," Rich Loc counted out five grand, folded it, and placed it in the dresser beside her bed. "That's five gees, right there. I'll hit chu with another five once you get outta here." He caressed her cheek and kissed her forehead. He went to walk away, but she grabbed his hand. "What's up?"

"Where are you going?"

"I'm finna bounce. I gotta few corners I gotta bend."

"I was hoping you'd spend the night with me."

"I would, ma, but I gotta get on this nigga ass that got away." Rich Loc went to kiss her, and she turned her head. "Oh, so it's like that? Check it, I'm not finna trip off you and yo lil funky attitude. You'll get over shit soon enough." He lifted her hand to his lips and kissed it tenderly. "I love you." Rich Loc made his way around the bed, tapping the end of it and walking toward the door.

Chapter 6

Cowboy, eyes closed, lay against the headboard, rubbing the injection site on the inside of his arm and licking his lips. He half listened to Golden as his high began to fade, uttering "unh huh" and "ummhmm" to whatever he said.

"Nigga, yo' ass ain't even listenin' to me." Golden smacked Cowboy upside his head, startling him. He sat up rubbing the stinging sensation at the side of his dome.

"Man, I oughta," Cowboy threw a few playful punches at Golden. Golden laughed and threw some back at him.

"Hold up, bro, lemme see who this is." Golden looked at his cellphone. His brows furrowed when he saw it was a blocked call, but he decided to answer it anyway. "Whuddup?"

"Ho ass nigga, you still alive?"

"What?"

"You heard me, bitch."

"Wait a minute, so that was you that hit my crib?"

"Yeah, that was my work. I missed, and I don't miss many."

"Fuck you coming at my neck for?"

"That stuff you gave me, one of the packages was sugar."

Golden turned around to Cowboy, who was frowning and listening to the conversation. Golden didn't know why, but something told him he had something to do with one of

Wood's kilos coming up short. Golden turned back around and focused his attention on his conversation with Wood.

"Nah, son, the shit I gave you was legit. I don't know what the fuck you talking about."

"Well know this, when I see you, it's up."

"Bet, fuck nigga." Golden disconnected the call. He was about to address Cowboy, but he got another call, so he answered it. "What up, pop? We're good. We're hangin' out at my lil spot. He's right here." He stole a glance at Cowboy, who was staring at him. "Okay." He extended his cellphone to Cowboy. "Pop wanna speak to you."

"Yeah?" Cowboy spoke into the cellphone. He was short and dry. "Baby bruh took care of me. I'm straight." The rest of the conversation was filled with a lot of "unh huh" and "yep."

"'Sup, old man?" Golden asked, taking the cellular from Cowboy. He massaged the bridge of his nose as he listened to what his father was telling him. "I hear you, pop, but I'm hot at ma and them right now. I'm talkin' blow torch hot. Right or wrong, they were 'posed to roll out for bruh."

"You're right, son. I can't even defend them for that," Heavy replied. "Just promise me that you'll get in touch with ya mother later tonight, or sometime tomorrow. You know how she gets when she's worried about one of y'all."

"A'ight, pop, I can fade that," Golden said. Then listened to what his father had to say. "I love you, too." He looked at Cowboy. "Pop, says he loves you, bruh." Cowboy nodded, but didn't say shit, so Golden lied on his behalf. "He said, he loves you, too. Okay. One." He disconnected the call and leaned forward, holding the cellphone. Cowboy could tell by the look on his face that he was thinking about something, and he was curious as to what.

"What's on yo' mind, G?" Cowboy inquired.

Golden took a deep breath. He sat up on the bed and turned around to Cowboy. "I need you to keep it tall with me,

31

big bruh. Did you swap one of the keys I sold to Wood with sugar?"

Cowboy stared at Golden for a minute. He could have lied to him easily, but he felt like he owed him for saving his ass that night. The way he saw it, telling him the truth was the least he could do.

Cowboy reluctantly nodded. "Yeah. It was me. I did that shit."

"Fuuuuck," Golden roared, hopping up from the bed and swinging at nothing. He ran his hand down his face and paced the floor. "Now we got funk with this nigga, Wood, and Rich Loc."

"Bruh, fuck the both of them niggaz. Once I heal up, we're at them boys' throats," Cowboy swore, watching Golden pace back and forth.

"I don't know where to start lookin' for Wood, but I can get at Rich Loc," Golden admitted. "Aries is stuck to him like a mouse to a sticky trap. All I gotta do is make the arrangement and blow his whole shit off."

"That reminds me," Cowboy started back up. "Did you have someone make a call to get that fool to leave the school? 'Cause it was like, as soon as dude left, you came in blastin'."

"Yeah. I had Aries make the call."

"Pardon my choice of words, but that was stupid."

Golden didn't say shit. He knew Cowboy was right.

"Wait a minute, you didn't lay homie down 'cause home-girl convinced you not to? She has feelings for this dick sucka, doesn't she?" Golden dropped his head when Cowboy looked at him. "Boy, boy, boy. You've got a problem on your hands, G."

"You think I don't know that?"

"You needa fall back from that bitch, kid. She doesn't know which one of y'all she wants. Shit, she may fuck around and hit chu with a whammy and whack you so she can be with 'em."

"I know, man, a nigga in a straight-up love triangle," Golden admitted, shaking his head. He knew he was a simp for allowing Aries to put him in such a situation.

"Look, bruh, you saved my life tonight, so I owe you one," Cowboy told him. "I know you ain't got it in you to kill ol' boy and yo broad, so big bruh gon' do you a favor, and execute both of their asses, once I'm feeling better. I gotchu, bro. You ain't got nothing to worry about," he swore, touching his fist to the left side of his chest.

Golden thought things over. He knew that his brother was right, and he wanted to give him the go-ahead to murk Aries and Rich Loc, but he feared he'd regret his decision. What he wanted to do was wait things out and see what Aries would do. He was aware that his waiting could end with him losing his life, but that was a risk he was willing to take.

"I'm going to take a rain check, bro, I'll let you know when and if I want you to make that move."

"Alright then, lil bruh, just lemme know," Cowboy slapped hands with Golden and embraced him. "I love you, nigga."

"I love you, too, big dawg."

Golden glanced at his timepiece and looked back up at Cowboy. "Yo, all that shit in the fridge has expired, so I'ma clean it out, and go get some groceries. You want anything specific?"

Cowboy shook his head no.

"A'ight, I'll be back in a minute." He touched fists with Cowboy and left the bedroom.

Cowboy thought about chastising Golden about the whole Aries and Rich Loc situation, but he knew how love could mess a nigga's head up, so he decided to fall back and let things play out. But if anything happened to Golden because of Aries, he was going to twist her and Rich Loc's cap back.

Chapter 7

The smell of a hearty breakfast made a sleeping Cowboy's nose twitch. His eyes fluttered open and he looked around, smacking his lips. Sitting up, he tilted his head back, yawning and stretching his arms. He slipped his feet into a pair of corduroy house shoes and rose from the bed, scratching his balls. He was as hungry as a hostage, and ready to devour whatever was being whipped up inside the kitchen.

A familiar voice singing Minnie Riperton's "Lovin' You" floated into the bedroom, along with the delicious aroma of the morning breakfast. Cowboy's brain finally recognized the food being prepared. It was a mixture of a ham and cheese omelet, with onions and bell peppers, bacon, and grits. And that beautiful, sultry voice, well, that belonged to his favorite girl. That belonged to his…

"Momma? What is she doin' here?" Cowboy wondered aloud. Fully alert, he slipped his undershirt over his head and slipped on a pair of gray sweatpants. Cowboy had the biggest smile on his face. He was so excited to see his mother. All of these years he thought she was dead, but she was alive. He couldn't believe it. It was like he had awakened from a nightmare.

She's alive. I can't believe it. She's alive, Cowboy thought. Although he smiled, his eyes were glassy and on the verge of tears.

"Momma, wait 'til I tell you about the dream I had. It was crazy," Cowboy said. He snatched the bedroom door open, dashed across the hall, and into the bathroom, where he washed his face and brushed his teeth.

Cowboy ran out of the bathroom so fast that he fell in the hallway. He scrambled back up to his feet, losing one of his corduroy house shoes in the process, and running down the corridor toward the kitchen. He held himself up in the kitchen doorway, breathing heavily, and staring at his mother's back. Chick was in a leopard print robe and furry slippers. She sang her heart out as she danced around the kitchen, whipping up breakfast.

Cowboy watched his mother, like she was performing at her sold-out concert. He couldn't stop smiling as tears of joy spilled down his cheeks.

"Momma," Cowboy called for his mother's attention. Holding the broom, pretending it was a microphone, Chick abruptly stopped singing and looked up at her only child.

Cowboy dropped to his knees and wrapped his arms around his mother's waist. Tears flooded his cheeks and snot oozed out of his nose. He held his mother tightly, afraid she'd disappear, like some sort of a mirage in the desert. He couldn't believe she'd been alive after all this time.

"Ma, I can't, I can't believe it really is you," Cowboy choked out between sobs, his voice thick with emotion. "I thought you were gone. I thought I'd lost you forever." He broke down sobbing harder, shoulders rocking, face buried in her torso. "Don't leave me, momma, don't leave me again, please. I feel so alone in this world."

Chick. His mother—no, not his mother, but his younger brother, Golden, whose waist he was holding, looked down at him teary-eyed. A combination of pity and concern was etched across his face. He was about to rub his older brother's head but hesitated for a moment. He wasn't sure if a form of affection would help or hurt his sibling's mental state. Then he thought about it for a minute. Cowboy needed to be comforted in this moment, so for now, he'd play along with his delusion.

Golden rubbed Cowboy's head with one hand and his back with the other. Cowboy laid the side of his face against his torso and closed his eyes. He came down from his sobbing and whimpered, like a child trying to sleep after a nightmare.

Golden cleared his throat and prepared to put on his best impression of a woman.

"I've gotchu, baby boy. Mommy's here. Mommy's here, and I'm not going anywhere, ever," Golden said softly, his voice gentle but tinged with sadness. "That's a promise."

"Momma."

"Yes, baby."

"Tell me you love me, please."

Golden shut his eyes and tears spilled down his cheeks. It hurt him to the very depths of his soul to hear his brother like this. Here was a man, who was the epitome of a gangsta. There wasn't a part of the game he hadn't experienced and conquered, but here he was now, reduced to a toddler, crying and begging to be loved by his mother. This told Golden that no matter how tough a nigga seemed on the outside, he needed to be loved and appreciated, like every human being.

Cowboy, with hope-filled eyes, looked up at Golden. "Momma?"

"Momma loves you, baby."

Cowboy smiled from ear to ear and laid the side of his face back against Golden. With his eyes closed, he said, "Momma, can you sing to me how used to when I was lil?"

"Sure. What would you like me to sing?"

"I don't know. Anything. I loved when you used to sing to me."

"Okay," Golden replied, caressing Cowboy's head. "Twinkle, twinkle, little star. How I wonder what you are. Up above the world so high, like a diamond in the sky…"

Golden sang until Cowboy was content and then they sat at the table to eat. He listened to his brother pour his heart out to his mother, telling her how much he missed her. How he prayed to God for his life to be a bad dream, and she'd come walking back up to their house. He started crying again, but this time he was smiling. He stuffed his face, while he told her everything that happened to him in her absence.

Golden played along with his brother's delusions. His heart broke for the man he used to look up to as his older brother. He knew Cowboy wasn't right upstairs. His mind was fractured and broken from losing his mother and dealing with all the traumatic experiences the street life brought. But for now, he would continue to pretend to be his mother, if only to give Cowboy some semblance of comfort amid his pain.

Golden could sympathize with Cowboy after hearing his plight. He understood why he went on a suicide missions to get money and pumped poison into his veins.

Golden got Cowboy to agree to have some tea with him. He turned his back to him as he emptied four crushed Ambien pills into his cup and stirred it. Cowboy was a pretty big dude so he was sure he could handle such a dosage.

"Here you go, baby boy," Golden passed him his cup of tea and sat beside him on the living room couch.

"What kind did you say this was again, momma?" Cowboy asked, taking a cautious sip of the hot beverage.

"Apple cinnamon, with just a splash of lemon." Golden grinned, as he sipped from his cup and watched him attentively.

Golden started rambling about a whole bunch of nothing, and before he knew it, Cowboy was dozing off. He struggled to keep his eyes open and his head upright, to no avail. He dropped the cup of tea and fell back on the couch, snoring. Golden sat his cup on the coffee table, removed his big brother's house shoes, and draped a blanket over him. Standing over him, he watched him sleep peacefully, and wondered what he was dreaming about, if he was dreaming.

"You're a pain in my ass, but I love you, you crazy muthafucka," Golden said, hoping his words were sinking into his brother's brain, while he lay asleep. "I swear on everythang I hold sacred, I'm gonna do everythang in my power to getchu the help you need. Lil bruh got a lot he's dealin' with right now, so just bear with me."

Golden would find a way to address Cowboy's mental illness and get him the help he so desperately needed. He vowed to be there for him and give him the solace he needed in the face of adversity.

Chapter 8

Cowboy walked into the backyard, where he saw Golden inside the garage. He was busy fixing something underneath the hood of a sandy-brown '68 Dodge Charger. Tupac's "Troublesome 96" was pumping so loud from the old boom box sitting on the ground that he didn't hear Cowboy walking up behind him. It wasn't until he saw his shadow at the corner of his eye that Golden noticed he wasn't alone. He snatched his gun from the top of the battery and swung it around to him. He was about to squeeze the trigger when he saw it was Cowboy. Sighing, he sat his piece back down and turned the volume down on the boombox.

"Big bruh, I almost popped yo' ass, thinkin' you an opp," Golden said, wiping the oil from his hands with a dirty red rag. He shook up with Cowboy and leaned against the Charger, tucking the rag inside his right back pocket. He watched as Cowboy walked around the old Charger, dragging his finger alongside it.

"I remember this car. This was Pop's first whip when he moved out here," Cowboy said, coming around the rear of the vehicle.

"Yeah, I recall. He taught me and you how to drive in it." Golden smiled, looking back at the steering wheel of the Charger, and seeing his ten-year-old self trying to drive.

"Man, we had some memories of this baby." Cowboy smiled, looking at the whip's interior through its back window.

"You ain't never lied. I got my first blow job in the backseat of her." Golden looked up at the ceiling, smiling and reminiscing.

Cowboy's face balled up angrily, when he locked eyes on the family photo wedged between the speedometer and the dashboard. His hatred for his family suddenly surfaced and reminded him of how much he wanted them dead.

Golden noticed his brother was staring at their family photo. He figured now was as good of a time as any to try to bridge the gap between him and his kinfolk. "You know Baby Girl and I got some get-back for you. We cleaned up Curtis and that bitch, Jade. Sis bumped home-girl, and made sure she knew it was on the account of the love she had for you," he said. When Cowboy didn't say anything, he went ahead and threw in something else. "I hollered at Big, too. He said he'd think about squashing the beef with ch…"

"Man, fuck the twins, fuck pop, and fuck yo' trife ass moms, too," Cowboy roared, spit flying from his lips. "You know yo' moms killed Chick?"

Golden looked shocked when he heard this.

"That's right, yo' moms killed my moms. I saw the shit with my very own eyes, too. She killed her, and pop helped her chop up the body and bury it in some fuckin' place. Where? I don't fuckin' know." Tears slid down his cheeks and his nostrils flared.

"Bruh, I, I, I," Golden stuttered, trying to say something. He was really at a loss for words. What could he possibly say in his mother's defense?

"You're at a loss for words, huh? I knew you would be," Cowboy said. "I would be, too, if I were in yo' shoes. But I'll tell you this, my nigga. I will right some wrongs and mothafuckaz will," Cowboy's voice changed to a more hostile feminine one, and his face appeared to transform. "Pay for what they've done to my son. I won't leave anyone alive that hurt my baby for 'em to try it again. Fuck that. Those mothafuckaz are gonna pay what they owe, one way or another. I swear on Cowboy's life."

Golden's eyes widened, hearing his brother's voice flip to a feminine one. What really got him was his face changing to look like an angry woman. The combination of his womanly voice and facial features was giving him demonic vibes, and he didn't like it at all.

"What the fuck?" Golden uttered.

Cowboy ran past Golden, bumping his shoulder, and entering the house through the backdoor. He slammed the door shut and disappeared somewhere inside the house.

***

After he was done fixing the Charger, Golden sat behind its wheel, smoking a blunt and thinking about what Cowboy told him. He wondered if all the heroin his brother had done over the years had finally gotten to his brain, or was he actually telling the truth? If he was keeping it one hundred, then he really didn't know his mother, like he thought he did. To kill a bitch and raise her son was some cold-ass shit.

I got so much shit on my plate that I'm already dealin' with. Now I've gotta add this to it, Golden thought, lying his head back against the headrest and blowing out smoke. He took a deep breath, mashed out his blunt, and hopped out of the car.

***

Golden slipped on his jacket as he walked up to Cowboy's bedroom door and knocked on it. He waited for the bedroom door to be opened, but he never came, so he knocked again. Golden figured Cowboy was still tight about earlier, so he wasn't going to press him.

"Yo, Cow, I got pop's old Charger runnin', and I left the keys on the kitchen table, in case you wanna take a drive to get chu a lil fresh air," Golden told him. "I also left you a few dollars on the table. I'm finna head back out to the city, so I'll get up witchu later. Love, bruh." He waited a moment longer for a response, but he didn't get one, so he left the house.

**

Cowboy sat on the bed with his back against the headboard, writing down a list of names. Once he couldn't think of anyone else to add to his list, he sat the ink pen on the nightstand and looked over it.

"You sure this is everyone?" Cowboy asked, in his mother's voice.

"Yeah. I'm sure that's everyone. Mommy, I really don't need you to go at these bustas' necks for me. I'm a grown man. I can get down for mine by myself."

He went on to reply in his mother's voice. "I'm fully aware you're grown, but you're still my baby. You've been puttin' it down for yo'self for some time, but now I'm here. So, fall back, son, and lemme show these ho-ass niggaz why they fucked with the wrong bitch's son."

He nodded. "A'ight, ma. Keep in mind, I've gotta slide by the old lady's house to get that money I stashed. I'd like to bless her family with a bag and put the rest up with a friend of mine."

"Alright, baby boy, it's your show for now."

"Thank you."

Cowboy's delusions led to him seeing his mother rubbing the side of his face and kissing him on the forehead. He smiled like a little boy getting two scoops of his favorite flavor of ice cream.

***

Wood's goons lounged around the garage, talking shit, while he sat in a worn La-Z-Boy sofa chair, sharpening his machete. Once he'd fashioned the blade to a razor's edge, he stood up, swinging it and thrusting it. He saw something in the corner of his eye and looked over his shoulder. A stray dog was snooping around for something to eat. He whistled for the animal's attention and waved it over, when it looked. Hopeful that Wood had food, the hound wandered over to him. Kneeling, Wood rubbed the dog's back and ruffled its head. Swiftly, he came from around his back with his machete and chopped the poor animal's head off.

"Now that's what I call sharp," Wood said to no one in particular, staring at his reflection in the blood-stained blade.

Remo and the goons inside of the garage stared at Wood, like he had a couple of screws loose. Wood turned to Remo and wiped the blood from the machete on his shirt. He looked at the horrified look on the goons faces and wondered what had them so uptight.

"What?" Wood asked, clueless.

Chapter 9

Aries was surprised when Rich Loc popped up at the hospital. She wasn't supposed to be released until tomorrow afternoon, and even then, she had it in mind to catch a Lyft to Golden's spot to spend some time with him, but Rich Loc had derailed that plan. He came into her room, demanding she get dressed so they could leave. He had a mad dog expression on his face and ignored any questions she asked. Aries could feel her blood pressure shoot through the roof. She wholeheartedly believed that he discovered the secret she'd been keeping and was going to make her pay for her betrayal.

The hospital's west wing hallway stretched like an endless tunnel. Its off-white walls were lined with abstract paintings that failed to distract Aries from the growing knot of anxiety in her stomach. Rich Loc's hardened demeanor and silent presence only served to intensify her unease, his tall stature cast a shadow over her as he guided her wheelchair with a forceful grip.

Aries's mind raced with a thousand thoughts. She didn't know what Rich Loc had in store for her, and fear of the unknown was driving her crazy.

"Babe, where are we going?" Aries's voice quivered, as her wheelchair rolled down the empty corridor. Glancing up at Rich Loc, she searched for any hint of reassurance in his impassive expression but found none.

Ignoring her question, Rich Loc forged ahead, his silence was a palpable barrier between them. Aries clenched her jaws and squeezed the armrests of her wheelchair. She was frustrated and fear was bubbling beneath the surface as they approached the elevator.

Aries's nurse, a Jamaican woman with dreadlocks that were nappy at their roots, came forward, with concern in her voice. "Suh, me need yew ta wait fuh da discharge paperwo—"

Rich Loc cut the chubby Caribbean woman off with a dismissive wave of his hand, his impatience evident by the look on his face. "We don't have time for no fuckin' paperwork," he snapped, his tone brooking no argument, as he maneuvered Aries inside the elevator.

Aries's heart thudded crazily in her chest, as the elevator's doors closed. The confined space amplified her sense of claustrophobia. The presence of a sheriff deputy only added to her growing sense of dread.

"Where are you guys headed?" the deputy asked, with his hand hovering over the panel's buttons.

"Garage," Rich Loc replied flatly.

The deputy pressed the G-button for the garage and the L-button for himself. He was going down to the lobby.

The deputy tried to make small talk with Rich Loc, asking him about the Lakers game and shit, but his conversation was dry. So, he figured he'd converse with Aries instead.

"I bet you're glad you can finally go home and sleep in a nice, cozy bed with your man, and eat some real food," the deputy said, thinking back to his hospital stay a couple of years ago. "This hospital food ain't but a step above the chow they serve you in the county."

"Y-yeah, you're right about that," Aries smiled weakly, and lowered her gaze. She unintentionally gave off battered wife vibes and the deputy picked up on it. His eyes flashed concern and his forehead wrinkled.

"Ma'am, are you alright?" the deputy placed his strong, vein-riddled hand on hers, as he posed the question.

Aries looked up at Rich Loc's reflection in the elevator door and met his evil glare. The look on his face told her she better not say the wrong thing, or there would be hell to pay.

"Uh, no, I'm fine, sheriff," Aries replied with another weak smile.

The deputy glanced up at Rich Loc, and he faked like he was studying the illuminated numbers above the elevator doors. He set his sights back on Aries, looking deep into her eyes.

"Are you sure?" he asked sternly, grasping her hand.

Right then, the elevator's doors slid open to the hospital's lobby, leaving the deputy's question lingering in the air. There was a strange silence as the law enforcer waited for her answer.

"Oh, yes, I'm fine, sheriff. I'm just a lil tired. That's all," Aries assured him. "You know you don't get much rest in these hospitals, with nurses and doctors runnin' in and outta yo' room."

The deputy nodded understandingly. A grin slowly emerged on his face. "I feel your plight. You folks take care and have a nice night."

The deputy walked out of the elevator and the doors closed behind him.

"I thought his good talkin' ass would never leave outta here," Rich Loc said, irritated. "Muthafuckin' pigs don't ever stop talkin'. Dead homies."

Aries's mind raced with a whirlwind of thoughts and emotions, when the sheriff's deputy inquired about her wellbeing. She knew she was in danger, but to reveal the truth to him would have led to deadly consequences. Rich Loc stayed strapped 24/7 and that night he was on one. So, if the deputy came at him, there would have been a shootout that would have ended with one, if not both, of them dead.

Aries knew that the sheriff's deputy had a family, and to put him in a situation that could cost him his life would have been selfish of her. So, she decided to keep her mouth shut and play the cards she was dealt. She knew that Rich Loc loved her, so if she found herself at the wrong end of his gun, she could use his affection for her to gain some sympathy that would make him spare her.

After bitching about the sheriff's deputy, Rich Loc reverted back to the strong and silent archetype. The elevator doors slid open to the parking garage, and Rich Loc guided Aries out. As Aries was ushered across the lot, she made a silent vow to escape her fiancé's sinister intentions.

***

Rich Loc parked at the back of a gentlemen's club called Papa's and recovered his gun from the stash box. Aries looked around nervously, wondering where she had been taken. Except for a black Mercedes-Benz Sprinter van, Rich Loc's whip was the only vehicle present.

"Babe, where are we going?" Aries asked.

Rich Loc had just slammed the door closed and was walking around to her side. Before she could lock the passenger door, he was snatching it open and pulling her out of the front seat. She nearly fell to the pavement, but he held fast.

Rich Loc speed walked through the parking lot towards the backdoor entrance of Papa's. He was walking so fast that Aries lost her balance and almost fell.

"Baby, what is this all about? What did I do?" Aries inquired, scanning the parking lot for anyone who could help her.

Rich Loc didn't say a damn thing. It was as if she was talking to a deaf man. He rapped on the thick iron door and stood aside, so the door wouldn't hit him. A few minutes later, he heard locks and latches coming undone, then the door was pulled open by Parelli. He was rocking a black T-shirt and a blue bandana around his neck. Cradling a choppa with a long strap, he scanned the parking lot, and then waved Rich Loc inside.

As soon as Rich Loc and Aries walked in through the backdoor, they heard the iron door being shut and its locks being done. Parelli walked ahead of them and they followed. He led them across the empty dance floor, past the bar, the stage, through the kitchen, into the back storage room, and finally, to a wall-to-wall refrigerator.

Parelli punched a combination in on the digital keypad outside the refrigerator door. There was a humming, the floor shook, and then what sounded like an elevator descending resonated. Parelli opened the refrigerator door and exposed a shelf of cold beverages. The shelf ascended into the ceiling and revealed a long corridor.

Parelli stepped into the corridor, with Rich Loc and Aries coming up behind him. The corridor was so quiet they could hear the flies swarming around the yellowish light bulbs in the ceiling. The bulbs flickered, as if they were going to cut off, but they never did. The walls were a dull green, with graffiti and amateur illustrations carved into them. It seemed like every five seconds a rodent was darting back and forth across the floor, disappearing inside one of many cracks in the walls.

"Aaaaaah," Aries hollered, nearly jumping into Rich Loc's arms, when a mouse darted across her foot. Parelli stomped the rodent and kicked it down the hall, where it deflected off the wall. The filthy creature landed on its back twitching.

"Cuz, we seriously gotta get a cat, or somethin' for all of these mothafuckaz runnin' back and forth in here," Parelli said to no one in particular. A droplet of brown water splashed on his shoulder, and he looked up at the ceiling. There was a hairline crack where the water had dripped from. "A cat and a plumber, loc."

Chapter 10

Rich Loc was silent the entire time Parelli bumped his gums. The hardened expression on his face remained, as he led Aries down the corridor.

Boom, boom, boom.

Parelli rapped on an iron door and waited for an answer. A moment later, the eye slot in the door drew back and a pair of eyes appeared. They took in everyone on the opposite side of the door then the eye slot slid shut. The locks came undone, along with a latch. A five-foot-five, stocky nigga with frizzy cornrows opened the door. He was wearing a black T-shirt and matching Chuck Taylors, with fat blue laces in them. He adjusted the strap of the choppa on his shoulder and stepped aside, so Parelli and them could enter.

Parelli walked through the door first, followed by Rich Loc and a nervous Aries. She swallowed the lump of fear in her throat and inched her hand towards the scalpel she tucked inside her waistband. The iron door slammed shut and startled her. She looked over her shoulder and the five-foot-five dude was locking and latching the door. Aries took in the room. It was the size of your average basement. A security system was set up at the north wall. There was a desk and an office chair in front of eight monitors. The monitors were connected to the surveillance cameras outside, which showed everything surrounding the establishment. The rest of the room had stacked boxes, broken furniture, and old kitchen appliances that had collected dust, and spider webs.

Ahead of Aries stood a brolic dude with a wide forehead and short dreadlocks. He was cradling a choppa and standing over a short, muscular Chinese man. The man had a shackle around his neck, while his wrists were shackled to a big brown leather belt around his waist. The chains to the shackles extended to the wall. Aries estimated the Chinese man to be anywhere from twenty to twenty-five years old. His hair was unkempt, and he had little facial hair to speak of. The laceration above his eyebrow and his swollen knuckles told Aries that when Rich Loc's goons came for him, he didn't come along without a fight.

"Get 'em up, and toss me yo' piece, big dawg," Rich Loc told the big brolic nigga with the short dreadlocks.

The brolic nigga tossed his choppa to Rich Loc and roughly pulled the Chinese fool up to his feet. "Get cho ass up."

Rich Loc threw his head to the side for the big brolic nigga to get out of the way. He then placed the choppa in Aries's hands and showed her how to hold it. "Make sure you got a firm grip on her, bitch kicks like a donkey with its nut sack caught in a mouse trap."

Aries nodded. She began to sweat, and her heart was racing. She knew what was expected of her, without Rich Loc saying it.

"You remember this dick sucka, baby? Take a real good look at 'em," Rich Loc said, pacing back and forth across the floor.

Aries took a good look at the Chinese man, like Rich Loc told her. The Chinese man held her glare with his head held high, prepared to accept whatever hand fate dealt him.

"This tight-eyed muthafucka looks familiar to you, baby? Huh?" Rich Loc inquired, standing aside and pointing at the Chinese dude.

Aries looked from the Chinese nigga to Rich Loc, then back again. She was sweating and her hands were clammy. She didn't know how the hell Rich Loc had managed to find a nigga that she had made up in her head. The only thing she could think of was she had given him a description of someone she'd seen in passing.

Damn, he looks like the nigga I made up down to the T, but if I lay 'em down, I'll be killin' an innocent man. I don't know if I can live with that on my conscience, Aries thought. She looked at Rich Loc. *If I say this nigga isn't the one, with how much he looks like the guy I described, then he may become suspicious of the story I gave 'em. Fuck.*

Aries' face balled up angrily and she nodded. "Yeah. That's him. I'll never forget his face."

The Chinese man scrunched his face. He couldn't believe Aries was lying on him. He went to say something, but she upped the choppa and sprayed him. He bumped against the wall and stumbled forward. Teary-eyed, Aries sprayed him again, and again. He fell awkwardly to the floor and lay on his side. He wheezed, and stared at her accusingly.

"I'm sorry," Aries mouthed to her victim.

He looked up at Rich Loc, whose shadow eclipsed him. Rich Loc pulled his gun from the small of his back and popped the Chinese man in his forehead, sealing his fate. Rich Loc turned around to Aries, tucking his piece. He pulled the blue bandana from his left back pocket and took the choppa from her. He wiped her fingerprints off the assault rifle and passed it to the brolic nigga.

"J-Bo, get rid of this stick," Rich Loc ordered. Then he turned to Parelli and homie with the frizzy cornrows. "P, Diamond, y'all dump this nigga somewhere nobody can find his ass. I'm not tryna add the Asian Mafia Klan to the list of fools we already have static with."

Rich Loc cupped Aries' face and looked into her eyes. "Yo, you straight, ma?"

Aries mustered a weak smile and nodded.

"Good. I'ma take you home, feed you, bathe you, and give you a full body massage, fit for a queen."

"I'd love that," Aries replied, kissing him.

Rich Loc led Aries out of the room and down the corridor. The smile slowly melted from her face and was replaced by sadness. She glanced up at the ceiling and mouthed to God, "Please, forgive me, Lord." When Rich Loc glanced back at her, she threw up her fake smile again. They then hopped on the elevator they had come down in and vanished without a trace.

***

Aries murdering the Chinese gangsta had her rattled. She couldn't think straight for shit. Everywhere she looked, she could have sworn she saw him, but whenever she turned around, he was gone. Rich Loc massaging her became sensual, so she knew where things were headed. At first, she started to stop him, because she wasn't in the mood, but then she thought that sex could potentially take her mind off the deadly sin she committed. With that in mind, she took a breath and released the tension from her body. As soon as she did, she felt his long, thick, thumping dick stretching her to her limits. She gasped underneath his deep, long, passionate strokes. Her kitty clenched and unclenched him.

Rich Loc laid down on Aries's back, slipping one hand underneath her to rub her clit. He grasped her neck with his other hand and talked dirty to her. Her face was a mask of bliss, as he punished her soaking wet pussy.

"Yeah, you like it like this, huh? You like for a loc to fuck yo' lil pretty ass like a savage?" Rich Loc said through clenched teeth, sweat bubbles oozing out of his pores. "You

53

wanna nigga to get balls deep, and hit the bottom of this muthafuckin' pussy, don't chu? Tell me?" he demanded, pumping faster and deeper inside of her.

"Oh, yes. Yes, I love it. Fuck me, baby, fuck me. Oooou." Aries's eyes rolled over, like she was having a seizure.

Rich Loc was fucking her so hard from the back that it sounded like a pistol being fired. His mound of pubic hair was smacking up against her buttocks and sending ripples through. Licking her top lip, she squeezed her eyes closed and started throwing it back at him. Their motions became in sync, as they matched each other stroke for stroke.

"Aaaah, shiiit. Aaaah, fuck," Rich Loc said with his eyes shut, biting down on his bottom lip, and throwing himself into her harder and faster. Shorty felt good as hell, and he was on the verge of busting but wanted to last at least five minutes longer.

"Unh hunh, this pussy feels good to you, huh? Makes you wanna bust, don't it?" Aries asked, looking over her shoulder at him, and flicking her tongue rapidly.

The sight had him aroused, and he could feel his little head swelling to a bulb.

"Yeah, ma, this pussy fie. I'ma, I'ma bust," Rich Loc replied softly. He wasn't doing anything, besides holding up his body weight, while little mama threw that pussy up at him.

"Where you gon' bust, pa? Tell mommy where you gon' bust."

"I'ma bust, I'ma bust all up in this muthafuckin' pussyyy." Rich Loc made an ugly face as he threw his head back. Hands-free, he pulled his shiny pipe out of Aries and rested it between the crack of her ass. His babies shot out in globs, plastering her dimpled buttocks and leaving them shiny and wet.

Rich Loc fell over on the bed on his back, staring up at the ceiling, with his chest heaving. He was hot and sweaty, but that nut he caught made it worth it. Aries lie on her stomach, like Manny Pacquiao when he got knocked out. Her eyes were shut, and a pleased smile was on her face. She felt down Rich Loc's chest until she discovered his dick, stroking that mothafucka. He got strong in her delicate grasp. The head of his piece was pulsating and running wet with a shiny essence.

Aries took him inside of her warm mouth, bobbing up and down his pole, massaging his balls. Eyes closed, Rich Loc smirked and ran his hand through her hair, listening to her slurping and sucking.

On God, I love my bitch. I'd die for this pussy, Rich Loc smiled like he'd been granted entrance to the Gates of Heaven by Jesus himself. Little did he know, his thoughts may come to real life.

Chapter 11

Golden was a man on a mission. He recalled Aries telling him Jade had dropped a dime on Cowboy for that hundred-thousand-dollar bag. He was certain Jade was shacked up with Curtis. He knew where old boy laid his head, too. He had planned on crushing him when he came home, so he made it his business to get his hands on his address. He would have been rocked the love-sick C.O. to sleep, but the recent events had side-tracked him. Tonight was as good a time as any to set that ass straight, though. Not only did he have the time, he had the right weaponry and opportunity.

Golden knew he would drop at least two bodies that night, so he had to get into that killa mindset. And what was a better way to get him in that mind frame than that old school, west coast gangsta shit? Spice 1's "Trigga Gots No Heart." Golden scowled as he spat the lyrics to the throwback track, sliding through the grimy streets of New York.

I'm sick up in this game
I'll take no secondary shorts-and
Slam dunk these bullets up in yo' chest like Jordan
Menace II Society mad man killer
Just call me the East Bay Gangsta
Neighborhood drug dealer

Golden's preparation for the night's mission was interrupted by a call from his sister. He turned the stereo down and answered his ringing cell.

"What up, sis?"

"Shit. I can tell you're in the streets. Where are you headed, bro?"

"To work."

Baby Girl was quiet for a moment, thinking about what he actually meant. "So, who is it that needs somethin' fixed?"

"CB's slide and her old man."

"Come scoop me. I'ma roll witchu."

"Nah. I got this."

"You got the last one, and I know you saw me tryna catch up witchu," Baby Girl told him. "I should kick yo' ass for leavin' me. You're lucky I love you, nigga. Listen, I'm not takin' no for an answer, come scoop me. I'm finna get ready."

Before Golden protested any further, Baby Girl hung up on him. He couldn't help smiling, thinking of how mannish she was at times. He thought about it for a second and decided he was going to go pick her up. He could use the extra muscle, in case shit proved to be too much for him.

***

Golden drove up in front of his mother's crib. He texted Baby Girl, and five minutes later, she jogged from the side of the house. She was cloaked in a hoodie two sizes too big and baggy jeans. He was certain her duds belonged to Biggie. Since they were kids, she had a habit of stealing his drip to wear to school, and then sneaking it back inside his closet later. She was a Tomboy back then, and her twin brother had swag and could dress his ass off. So, Golden couldn't blame her. If he were in her shoes, he'd probably do the same.

Baby Girl directed Golden to the armory, fifteen minutes away from their mother's house. The armory was where they kept most of their weapons and protective gear. They had a few of these spots scattered throughout the five boroughs, in case they ran into some trouble and needed to get their hands on a gun.

"Who are these people we're goin' after again?" Baby Girl asked, slipping on a Kevlar bulletproof vest.

"You know that bitch Jade that Cowboy bangs needles with? Well, she dimed 'em out to that nigga Rich Loc for six figures."

Baby Girl looked surprised to hear who betrayed her oldest brother. "I know you're fuckin' lying."

"As fucked up as it is, sis, I wish I was, but it's the truth, unfortunately," Golden assured her, adjusting his Kevlar bulletproof vest.

Baby Girl wore a mad dog expression as she shook her head. She always thought that Jade loved her brother, but apparently, she loved money more.

Baby Girl picked up the AR-15 assault rifle with the infrared laser beam and swung it around to different areas inside of the bedroom. She pretended to take out any threats moving in to stake a claim on her and her brother's lives.

"Promise me that when we get there she's all mine, bro. This is some female-on-female type shit. This lil junkie bitch gotta pay what she owes. Ya feel me?"

Golden was silent as his only sister talked to him and handled the assault rifle. He'd seen her in action time and time again, so he knew she was fully capable of handling firearms. It just fucked him up that the same little girl that used to follow him around, begging to be taken to the store, was now performing like a female Rambo.

"I feel you, sis, and don't worry, you got that. That's my word." He hoisted his AR-15 assault rifle over his shoulder and dapped her up.

"Come on, bro-bro," Baby Girl tapped Golden as she walked toward the door. He followed her out of the bedroom, flipping the light switch off.

***

Curtis was so happy about the bag Jade had gotten from dropping a dime on Cowboy that he decided to give her three more days of getting high, before checking her into a rehabilitation clinic.

While a hundred bands were looked at as peanuts by some, to Curtis it was as good as a million dollars. Hell, it would take him nearly three years of punching the clock down at the prison before he was able to see that kind of cheese, so to get it all in one night was nothing short of a blessing. Jade had counted at least five times that he'd counted the money, by hand, since they'd gotten it. And when she'd excuse herself from the table so she could get high, his happy ass was working on the sixth.

Hearing knocking at the door of his mobile home, Curtis grabbed the black garbage bag Jade had been given the money and began sweeping stacks of cash into it.

"Just a second," Curtis shouted to his guests.

He'd invited over Bruce, Lionel, Joelle and his girlfriend, Bria. This was the clique. They'd been hanging together since Bedford Academy High, and now they were working together at the prison.

"Hell you and Jade doin' in there? Fuckin'?" Bruce laughed.

"I hope not, 'cause if so, I know it smells like turtle tank water in that muthafucka," Lionel chimed in, laughing.

"You niggaz watch y'all mouths, if you wanna keep all ya teeth," Curtis threatened. He didn't mind his buddies clowning him, but Jade was off limits.

Once Curtis had swept all the money into the garbage bag, he tied it up and tossed it inside of the hallway closet. He took the time to straighten the wrinkles out in his shirt, took a breath and opened the door for his guests. Everyone walked inside, exchanging pleasantries and shaking up with Curtis. Curtis had invited them over to play Spades. Although he didn't need their money, he knew they wouldn't be interested in playing if there wasn't any cash on the line.

Curtis sat back down at the living room table, where Joelle and Bria were already sitting. Bruce and Lionel were inside the kitchen, helping themselves to the cold beers, sandwiches and chips on the counter. The burly men had packed their plates with enough food to feed three people. Curtis grinned and shook his head, seeing the piles of sandwiches and chips they had. He didn't mind how much the men ate; he was only interested in the memories and good times he was sure to have with them that night.

"Yo, Curt, where's Jade?" Bruce asked, with a mouth full of food. He'd just sat at the table with his plate and two beers.

"Takin' a shit," Curtis said, doing tricks with the playing cards. He'd lied needlessly, because everyone present was well aware of Jade's heroin addiction. Still, he wouldn't feel right telling them she was in the bathroom shooting dope.

Chapter 12

"Damn, Curt, you don't see niggaz eatin'?" Lionel frowned with a cheek full of food, heading out of the kitchen.

"Well, hell, Bruce asked," Curtis told him.

"True. But you coulda told 'em in a way that didn't make me picture turds splashin' into the toilet water. You inconsiderate fuck!" Lionel frowned, passing Bria the Heineken she requested while he was fixing his plate.

"Thanks, bro." Bria popped the cap and took a swig.

"Aye, muthafucka!" Bruce mad dogged Joelle after he'd snatched one of his beers.

"Shut up, fat boy. You don't need two of 'em anyway," Joelle grinned, popping the cap on the beer with the opener on his key ring.

Bruce snatched his prison issued gun from the holster on his hip and pointed it at Joelle's face. "I should give yo' black ass an extra eye for that shit."

"Play witcha self, but don't play with my man," Bria interjected, pointing her prison-issued gun at him. She was clutching her weapon with both hands.

"Whewww. Joe got 'em self a rider on the team," Curtis laughed, rocking back and forth on the hind legs of his chair.

"My bad. I don't want no trouble," Bruce stuck his gun back inside its holster.

"Thanks for always havin' my back, baby." Joelle kissed Bria.

"Thanks for always havin' my front," Bria said.

Bruce rolled his eyes and popped a potato chip in his mouth.

"Alright, ladies, let the games begin," Curtis dished out the cards.

***

Jade sat sideways on the toilet, facing the sink. Her eyes were filled with hunger as she held the flame below a worn, curved spoon. She licked her ashy lips, as the dope cooked in the silverware, reflecting in her pupils.

***

Golden and Baby Girl pulled their bandanas up around their noses. Baby Girl acted as a lookout, while Golden recovered their AR-15 assault rifles and a propane tank out of the trunk. They speed-walked up the sidewalk, keeping their eyes peeled for any nosey mothafuckaz that may be watching. Hunched down, the brother and sister duo invaded the yard of Curtis's mobile home. Golden sat the propane tank against the front door of the mobile home. Then he gave Baby Girl a thumbs up and motioned for her to go around back. She replied with a nod and retreated alongside the mobile home.

Golden peered through the window and took a head count of everyone present. He didn't see Jade but Curtis and his funkie, Joelle, were present. He figured they'd have to do for now, so he gently tapped on the window with his AR-15 and retreated to the center of the yard.

Bria opened the front door of the mobile home and it banged against something. Frowning, she tried to open the door wider, but found it difficult. She looked through the crack of the door and saw Golden aiming his assault rifle in her direction. It clicked inside her head that whatever he had his sight set on was flammable. Her eyes bubbled. She gasped. He pulled the trigger.

Boom. Frooosh.

The front of the mobile home exploded, and Bria flew backwards. She slammed into the wall, landing on her side, wide-eyed and dead. Burning cash and some that weren't ruined went up toward the ceiling and floated back toward the floor.

***

The explosion shook the bathroom, knocking Jade and several hygiene products to the floor. She shook off her dizzy spell and picked herself up. She untied the tourniquet and snatched the syringe out of her arm. Hearing someone running on the side of the mobile home, she sneakily peered out of the bathroom window. Baby Girl, clutching her AR-15 assault rifle, ran past the bathroom window, ignorant of her presence. Jade waited until she was out of sight and climbed out the window. She'd made it halfway out of the window before losing her bearings and falling awkwardly on her back.

Grimacing, Jade got back up and ran away, holding her lower back. Hearing automatic gunfire, she glanced over her shoulder and picked up the pace. She didn't know what was going on in the mobile home but she didn't want to get caught up in it. Besides, she didn't love Curtis enough to risk losing her life over him.

***

Using the butt of her AR-15 assault rifle, Baby Girl broke out the back bedroom window and punched out the remaining shards in its frame. She climbed through the window frame and stepped down onto the broken glass. She opened the bedroom door and moved down the hallway strategically. Smoke billowed out of the living room into the hallway. Approaching the living room, Baby Girl saw silhouettes running back and forth. She also heard coughing and gagging. She crossed the threshold inside of the living room, knocking shit down. Screams and hollers mixed with the crackling of the fires.

Baby Girl identified the two bodies she'd laid down as Joelle and his bitch, Bria. She knew there were more occupants to dispatch so she started to make her way around the room. Hearing a footstep at her rear, she swung around to blow away whoever was trying to creep up on her. She lowered her assault rifle when she saw it was Golden.

"I got this. Go catch up with shorty," Golden threw his head toward the doorway. Baby Girl looked through the doorway and saw Jade running across the front lawn.

Baby Girl dapped up and touched fists with Golden. Cradling her AR-15 assault rifle, she sprinted across the living room and disappeared through the doorway. She jumped down into the grass and chased after Jade.

With his sister out of his hair, Golden moved through the living room, stepping over dead bodies, in search of Curtis. When he didn't see Curtis among the expired, he knew he was lurking somewhere inside the mobile home. He didn't know what it was, but something told him Curtis was holed up in the master bedroom. As soon as the thought entered his mind, Golden upped his stick and sprayed the outside wall of the master bedroom. He listened closely for movement, but he didn't hear anything, so he sprayed the wall twice more.

"Muthafucka probably dead," Golden said under his breath, taking cautious steps toward the master bedroom. He wasn't aware of Curtis creeping up on him. He was wearing an oxygen mask and clutching a pistol grip automatic shotgun. He stepped over the dead bodies, as quietly as he could. Once he'd gotten within spitting distance of Golden, he lifted his shotgun, intending to blow his head off.

Golden reached for the knob of the master bedroom's door and saw a shadow on the wall at the corner of his eye. He dove out of the path of the shotgun as it ripped through the air. A big ass hole appeared in the wall, like a portal to another dimension. Curtis engaged the couch, letting his shotgun spit round after round, knocking the cotton out of it. Golden lay on the opposite side of the couch on his side. He had his assault rifle held up to his chest, trying to figure out his next move.

Bloom, bloom, bloom.

Curtis blew chunks out of the couch, sending cotton flying everywhere. Golden sat up on the floor and looked through the hole in the back of the couch. He could see Curtis approaching to blow him off the face of the earth. Golden stuck his weapon inside the hole in the back of the couch and squeezed the trigger.

"Ugh," Curtis grumbled as he took some hot shit through his belly. It felt like he'd been hit with a raging ball of fire. Dropping his automatic shotgun, he staggered backward, holding his bleeding stomach, like he had to take a dump. He looked at his hands and his palms were bloody. When he looked at the couch, Golden came up from the front of it and gave him a chest full.

Curtis stumbled backward fast, bumping into Joelle's dead body and falling flat on his back. He lay wheezing, like he needed a few puffs of an asthma pump. Golden walked up to him confidently. He knew he had Curtis by the balls and there wasn't any way he could get loose.

Golden stared down at the face-shield of Curtis's oxygen mask. He could see himself standing over the corrections officer with his assault rifle pinned on him. With a bloody finger, Curtis crossed his chest in the sign of the holy crucifix and awaited his send-off.

Blatatatatat.

***

Jade had made it halfway across her front lawn, when she heard movement at her back. When she peered over her shoulder, she saw Baby Girl chasing after her. Jade started screaming and crying for help.

Baby Girl was quickly closing the distance between them. Jade had cleared the residential street onto the other side, while Baby Girl had only made it halfway across it. An abrupt light from over her shoulder called for her attention. She looked to find a Ford Focus coming at her. Before she could avoid the car, it slammed into her, and she went flying over its windshield. She landed on her back and her assault rifle fell a few feet away from her. She bawled and held her back. The Ford Focus sped away.

Gritting, Baby Girl picked herself up from the pavement and grabbed her AR-15. By the time she turned around, Golden was running up to her with a warm assault rifle and concern in his eyes.

"Damn, sis, you good?" Golden asked, grasping her shoulder.

"Man, hell naw. My back hurtin' like a muthafucka," Baby Girl complained, rubbing her aching back.

"Come on. We better get outta here," Golden replied, pulling her along and looking around for any witnesses.

***

Golden drove away from the chaos he and Baby Girl created back at Curtis's place. Baby Girl frowned as she scoped out the neighborhood, hoping to see Jade, so she could finish her off.

Now if I was a dopefiend, where the hell would I go? Baby Girl thought, AR-15 lying across her lap.

Chapter 13

Jade's withdrawal from the dope was wreaking havoc on her body, and she was in dire need of getting it in her system. She could only think of one place that could set her straight, and she was on her way there now.

Jade walked up to the front door of an old three-story house that looked like it belonged on a horror movie poster. She knocked on the door in a distinct pattern, waited a few moments, and then knocked two more times. A moment later, she heard the chain being removed and the locks coming undone. The door opened and a blob of a man stood before her. He was tall, light-skinned, and rocked his reddish-brown hair in six cornrows. He wore a tan Dickie suit short-set, with the shirt open to show his wife beater. He held a big black semi-automatic shotgun over his shoulder, like a baseball player would a baseball bat.

"Grizz, what's up, big fella?" Jade asked.

Bear frowned when he noticed Jade was missing a leg and one of her pants legs was bloody. "Yo, what the fuck happened to you?"

"It's a long story. I'll—I'll tell you about it after I finish getting high."

"What's in the ice cooler?" Grizz nodded to the portable ice cooler in her other hand.

"You know, big fella, I never took you for a nosy mothafucka," Jade replied, wiping her sweaty brow.

"Look, for all a nigga know, you could have a bomb or something in that bitch. You're not getting up in here 'til I see what's in there."

"Fine," Jade said with irritation and shoved the ice cooler into his protruding belly. He leaned his shotgun up against the doorway, took the ice cooler into both hands and opened it. He made a disgusted face and fought back the urge to throw up. He had seen Jade's severed foot lying on a pile of ice cubes. Grizz closed the ice cooler and gave it back to her.

"Ya see what being nosy gets ya?" Jade asked nonchalantly.

Grizz picked his shotgun up and motioned her in with it. "Come on in, Jade."

Grizz shut the door behind Jade, once she stepped inside the house. She watched as he chained the door, locked about eight locks, and lowered an iron 4 x 4 across it. He then turned his back towards the door with his shotgun cradled in his arms. He posted up like one of the guardsmen of Buckingham Palace.

Jade began her stride taking in her surroundings. The room was big and spacious, like one of those dance studios where ballet class is held. All of the walls had been knocked down and there wasn't any furniture. It was just wall-to-wall hardwood floor. Jade's face twisted with disgust as she gagged from the overwhelming odor of blood, urine, and shit. She'd come into contact with the foul stench more times than she cared to remember, and she'd never grown used to it. She held her breath as she continued her journey through the dilapidated house. The four walls that made up the house were covered in graffiti and Rebirth was written over it in diarrhea that had dried over time.

There seemed to be fiends all around, and thanks to their drug of choice, they didn't look human at all. They were skinny with blemished skin and sores on their faces and around their mouths. Scabs and track marks covered their arms and legs. They looked like the creatures of someone's nightmare. The poor, lost souls were busy shooting heroin, preparing to shoot heroin, or bargaining with someone to get some of theirs.

Jade could hear many of the junkies whispering about the heroin called Rebirth that had taken hoods by storm. It was the recent craze among the fiends. They were willing to do any and everything they could to get their hands on the stuff. And as of now, this shooting gallery was the only place it could be purchased.

I'd bet my left titt this is what Hell looks like, Jade thought, taking an awkward step and falling to the floor. Looking up, she locked eyes with a haggard-looking dope-fiend with sores covering her face. Her new growth had pushed her burgundy weave up from her roots. Her long wrinkled breasts knocked against each other, as a D-boy fucked her doggy style. He was a young dark-skinned kid, sporting a New York Knicks cap backwards. His New York Knicks Jersey was pulled over the back of his neck, showcasing his bare chest and gold chain. The chain jumped up and down with each thrust he gave the dope-fiend. He threw his head back and bit down on his bottom lip. Anyone looking could tell by the expression on his face he was about to nut. The D-boy's grunting and the fiend he was fucking moans filled the air. Other fiends seemed to be shuffling around like zombies, talking to themselves or arguing over dope.

Jade approached a three-inch thick iron door with an eye-slot and tray at the bottom of it. She knocked on it, and its eye-slot slid open. A pair of intimidating eyes appeared and peered into her soul.

"What's up, Jade?" the man behind the door asked in a deep baritone voice.

"How—how're you doing, Tatt?" Jade asked. She appeared to be sweating more now. She'd gotten so sweaty and pale that she looked like she had come down with a fever.

"Oh, here we go with all this small talk and shit. I already know what the fuck that means," Tatt replied with a hostile demeanor. "Check this out, baby girl, that credit shit witchu is dead. We axed that shit. From now on, if you don't kick in some cash, I don't have no dope for yo ass."

"But Tatt, I—" Jade said as she rushed towards the door. She was cut short when Tatt slammed the eye-slot shut on her.

Jade pulled out everything in her pockets and accidentally dropped a couple of coins. When she looked in her palms, she had lint, a mangled stick of gum, and a few pennies. "Shit. I can't even cop a bag with this."

She cast the worthless items aside and looked at her right hand. She had a gold promise ring accented with a cubic zirconium diamond. Her son's father had given it to her years ago, along with his word to marry her within a year's time. She wished she knew better than to fall for the slick words of a low-life pimp. It would have saved her purity and, arguably, her greatest heartbreak. The only reason she'd kept the ring was because she had gained too much weight to get it off. But since she'd been on dope, she was sure she had lost enough weight to finally get it off her finger.

Jade tried to pull her promise ring off her finger, but it wouldn't budge. She sucked her ring finger making sure to get it sloppy wet. She tried to pull the ring off again and it slipped right off. Smiling, she held it up before her eyes and kissed it. She knocked on the iron door again, and the eye-slot was yanked open.

"You again?" Tatt asked, huffing his frustration.

"Before you turn a deaf ear to me, hear me out, Tatt," Jade told him as she held up her ring with both fingers. "This is a gold promise ring my trifling ass baby daddy gave to me some time ago. Now the diamond isn't real, but that gold is 14k."

"A'ight, lemme take a look at it," Tatt said.

She placed the ring down into the slot below. He pulled the eye-slot back shut and picked up the promise ring. Jade looked up at the ceiling, whispering to God with her hands together in prayer. She desperately needed Tatt to get her right.

As soon as she heard the bottom slot open, Jade walked up to the door and looked down into the slot. She smiled when she saw a handful of small bags of dope. She pocketed the drugs and went to the far corner of the room to get high. Along the way, she heard the fiends still chatting about the heroin. She felt like she'd hit the lottery, being she'd just come up on some.

Jade kicked the balled-up pieces of trash out of the corner, laid her jacket over the space she'd made, and sat on top of it. She removed everything she needed to get high from her fanny pack, laid it on her lap, and began preparing her fix.

Biting down on the syringe, Jade tied her tourniquet around her arm and tapped her inner arm, until a vein rose. Holding the flame of her Bic lighter below the marred spoon, she watched closely as the dope bubbled like boiling water. She dropped a piece of cotton into the spoon and let it soak up the heroine.

Afterward, she stuck the needle of the syringe into the moist piece of cotton and pulled it back into the feeder. Once the cotton sitting in the liquid dope was nearly dry, she eased the syringe into her vein. As soon as her blood mingled with the drug, a burgundy cloud formed. Jade pushed down on the feeder and released the highly addictive heroin inside of her bloodstream. Instantly, her eyes flickered and she grinned with satisfaction. Eyes shut, she watched the vibrant streaks of color zip back and forth across her eyes, while she listened to the bells and whistles. The grin dissolved from her lips, and she started doing the dope-head lean.

A rat snooped around Jade's sneaker for something to eat, and then scurried away to appease its appetite.

Chapter 14

Baby Girl went virtually unnoticed as she drifted through the shooting gallery. She was dressed in a baseball cap and army jacket, so she blended in perfectly with the lost souls, partaking in their poison of choice. This was exactly how she wanted it. The fewer people who witnessed what she was about to do, the better chance she had of getting away with it. Baby Girl located Jade far off in the corner by herself, shooting dope. She brushed the shoulders of fiends as she hurried in her direction, pulling a tourniquet from out of her jacket's pocket. She wrapped each end of the tourniquet around her fists and crept up behind her victim. She was in a dope nod and scratching the inside of her arm.

Swiftly, Baby Girl slipped the tourniquet around Jade's neck and yanked it tight against her chest. Jade's eyes bulged and she gagged. She tried to slip her hands under the tourniquet, but that only made Baby Girl pull tighter. Her eyes teared and globs of spit hung from her chin. She kicked fast and hard, scarring the already ruined hardwood floor.

"Cowboy sends his regards," Baby Girl whispered into Jade's ear, coldly. Hearing that made Jade fight even harder. It was like she knew she was definitely going to be a dead woman now. She twisted, turned, and tried to claw out Baby Girl's eyes, to no avail. Baby Girl, still strangling Jade, took a quick look at her surroundings. Her murdering Jade seemed to be going unnoticed by everyone.

Baby Girl focused her attention back on Jade. Her eyes fluttered. Her movements gradually grew slower. She took her last breath and her arms fell at her sides. She stared out the corners of her eyes, mouth hanging open in a grotesque manner. She'd expired.

Baby Girl wiped away the sweat dripping from her brows, removed the tourniquet from around Jade's neck, and stuffed it inside her pocket. She slumped Jade's body in the corner and placed her baseball cap over her face. If anyone saw her, they'd believe she'd fallen asleep.

From over her shoulder, Baby Girl scanned her surroundings, to make sure there weren't any eyes on her. Once she thought she was in the clear, she hopped up and walked away, with her head down.

***

It took some time, but Baby Girl was able to convince Golden to crash at their mother's place, instead of taking up residence at one of the armories. She tried to coerce him into sneaking back in through her bedroom window, but he wasn't having it. He reasoned he wasn't some teenager sneaking out to some party against his parents' wishes. He was a grown man in his mid-twenties, so if he was going to stay the night at his parents' house, then he was going to enter through the front door, like the rest of the adults that lived there. Baby Girl understood where her brother was coming from, so she didn't protest any further. She knew she'd sleep better that night, knowing most of her family was under one roof, so she agreed to let him have his way.

As soon as Baby Girl locked the front door behind Golden, they heard someone clapping and the living room light popped on. For a moment, she and Golden looked like a couple of deer caught in someone's headlights, but then things registered. Shirvetta and Biggie were sitting on the couch waiting for her return. Shirvetta had a colorful knitted blanket draped around her shoulders and a glass of wine in her hand. Biggie, on the other hand, was in a black do-rag and matching tank top, sucking on the end of a blunt. Baby Girl didn't know how long they'd been up waiting for her, but she got the feeling it had to have been a while.

Shirvetta swallowed the last of her wine before she addressed her only daughter. "And where have you been, young lady?"

"Big bro and I stepped out to handle some business," Baby Girl replied, pulling the hood off her head.

"Was this the kinda business that's gon' net this family some more cash?" Shirvetta asked.

"Nah," Golden chimed in. "We hadda go handle a family issue. This was personal, nothin' about checkin' a bag." He walked out of the kitchen, popping the top off a Heineken and tossing it in the trash.

"I'm guessin' it had somethin' to do with Cow," Biggie asked, dumping blunt ashes in an ashtray on the coffee table.

Golden, who was posted up against the wall, nodded. He had a frown on his face, thinking back to when he asked his family to roll out to rescue Cowboy and they declined. The thought of them not riding made him hot all over again. Truthfully, he wanted to beat his momma and his little brother's asses, so he had to check himself before he flew off the handle.

Baby Girl plopped down on the couch beside Biggie and he passed her his blunt. She went on indulging in the finest weed the five boroughs had to offer, while listening to their mother.

"Well, if that's the case, you and yo' brother needa peel outta those clothes, so I can burn 'em in the furnace," Shirvetta said. "Then you both needa scrub yo' tails thoroughly." She slipped off the blanket as she rose from the couch, outstretching her hand for their clothes. "Come on now. This is not y'all first dance. You know the procedure."

Golden took another swig of his beer and sat it down on the coffee table. Baby Girl excused herself to get undressed, while he did his duty there in the living room. Once he was done, he passed the clothes he'd broken the sixth commandment in to Shirvetta and she stuffed them inside a black garbage bag.

"I know you dumped whatever car you and yo' sister sinned in, so how'd y'all get back here?" Shirvetta wondered.

"We caught a ride from Granddaddy," Golden told her.

"Granddaddy?" Shirvetta frowned, wondering who he was talking about.

"Yeah. Not cho pops, but the old fiend that be drivin' dope boys to deliver work."

"Ma, he's talkin' about Grady," Biggie chimed in.

Shirvetta knew who Golden was talking about then. "You trust that old man to keep his mouth shut, son?" Shirvetta asked, looking in his eyes.

"Yeah. I threw the old head a few dollars, and told 'em to do exactly that," Golden told her. "He said he minds the business that pays 'em. Plus, he knows how the Loves give it up."

Shirvetta nodded her understanding. Baby Girl nudged her mother, and she took her clothes, stuffing them inside the black garbage bag.

Golden picked up his beer from the coffee table and walked toward the hallway. "I'm finna hop in the shower, and then I'm goin' to sleep."

"Golden," Shirvetta called for her son's attention, as she walked toward him. He turned around, raising his eyebrow. "I apologize for not comin' witchu to rescue your brother. Regardless of what Biggie said, I still should have accompanied you. Now I know I didn't give birth to Cowboy, but in my eyes, he's just as much of my son as he is your father's." She kissed him on the cheek and hugged him with her free arm.

Golden thought back to what Cowboy said about Shirvetta wasting his mother. He wanted to ask her if it was true, but thought it was better if he brought it up later. As much as he didn't want to believe his brother, he knew what some women were capable of doing behind a man they loved. His mother wasn't exempt. However, she was innocent until she was proven guilty. She would have to wait for her chance to stand trial because, right now, he wasn't in the mood.

"You forgive me, baby?" Shirvetta asked, her hand on his cheek.

Golden stared into his mother's eyes and believed she was sincere. "Yeah, ma. I forgive you."

Smiling, Shirvetta kissed and hugged her second oldest son again. She then turned to Biggie, who was back to sharing his bleezy with Baby Girl. "Biggie, you got something you wanna say to your brother?" she asked, giving him a look that said she wanted him to apologize for not going on the rescue mission with Golden.

Biggie shook his head, as he blew out a cloud of smoke. "Nah. I'm standin' on business, ma. Eff Cowboy. I know G in his feelings right now, but he'll eventually get over it."

Shirvetta gave Biggie the evil eye as she twisted her lips. She mouthed, "I should come over there and smack your head off your shoulders."

Biggie shrugged and went back to sharing his blunt with his twin.

"He'll come to his senses in time, baby. Just give 'em a minute. Okay?" Shirvetta said, rubbing Golden up and down his arm.

Golden stole a glance at Biggie, before walking back to his bedroom. Once he was gone, Shirvetta smacked Biggie upside his head, as she walked toward the basement. Angry, he looked over his shoulder at his mother, while Baby Girl snickered and coughed from the weed smoke.

"Man, twin, you needa getcho mama, for real." Biggie said, blunt pinched between his fingers.

"Oh, now she's just my mama, now that she made you mad, huh?" Baby Girl asked.

"Yep. Yours and Golden's," Biggie replied, before taking a few pulls. "Yo, twin, I'ma need you to slide with me to see if I can dump this Lamb tomorrow. You got me faded?"

Baby Girl nodded as she took the bleezy from him. "Yeah. That ain't 'bout nothin'.'"

"Cool," Biggie said, picking up the remote and turning on the flat screen. He pulled up the Netflix app to see what comedies they had on deck. Everything was funnier to him when he was high.

***

Golden removed his wife beater, stepped out of his boxer briefs, and eased into the hot sudsy water. Lying his head against the wall, he closed his eyes and took an exasperated breath. He'd been on the go since he touched the town and needed a break from everything and everyone. So tomorrow, he was going to take himself out to dinner, catch a movie, shop, get a mani and spend the rest of his day in someone's nice ass hotel.

Yep. Tomorrow is my day off, and I'm treating myself like a bad bitch a nigga tryna fuck.

Chapter 15

Remo was still hot about the way Wood handled him the night he discovered one of the bricks was sugar. He tried to put the violation at the back of his mind, but it kept coming to the forefront. He was waist-deep in his feelings, and he couldn't help it. Wood had treated him like he was a purebred ho, and he was far from that. The way he looked at it, his gangsta was just as official as Wood's, so he deserved the utmost respect, also.

"Yeah, son, nigga got anotha thang comin' if he thinks I'ma just lay down, after the way he played me," Remo said behind a surgical mask. He was wearing latex gloves, as he stood over the stove, cooking cocaine.

"You know how the big homie is when he's off his meds. Hell, we all know," one of Wood's workers said from the kitchen table. He was busy licking a blunt closed. "If I were you, I'd charge that shit to the game, bro."

Remo shook his head. He wasn't feeling how dude said he should handle the situation at all. "Nah, yo, I let this slide, and dude gon' make a habit out of it, any time he gets heated. Nah mean?"

The worker took the time to light up his blunt before replying to Remo. "I hear you, son, but that's the big homie."

Remo whipped around from the stove and launched the jar he was making crack in at the wall. The worker ducked the jar and it exploded against the wall. He looked up at Remo like he'd lost his goddamn mind.

"Maybe he's your big homie, but he ain't mine. Not anymore," Remo replied, removing his surgical mask and latex gloves. "Yo, man, I'm finna go get some pussy to get my mind right. You finish cookin' up the rest of this shit."

Remo walked past the worker, tossing the surgical mask and latex gloves inside the trash can on his way out of the kitchen.

"I can't wait to hear what this nigga, Wood, says when I tell 'em this shit," Trell said as he walked across the kitchen, grabbing the broom. He nearly shit his pants when he turned around and saw Remo pointing a gun at him.

Blowl, blowl, blowl!

Trell fell back against the refrigerator and slid down to the floor. He sat staring out the corners of his eyes with his mouth open.

"And to think, I was gon' put chu on a winnin' team," Remo shook his head.

Kneeling down, he checked Trell's pulse to make sure he was dead and tucked his piece at the small of his back. He picked up the blunt Trell dropped when he popped him and stood back up. He looked over the kitchen, while taking pulls and blowing smoke. He knew he had his work cut out for him, and he had to perform the tasks quickly. There wasn't any doubt in his mind someone had called the cops, and they were on their way there.

Remo made the kitchen look like niggas had kicked in the backdoor and robbed the cookhouse. He grabbed a pillowcase from one of the bedrooms and dumped the birds they were supposed to cook in it. He also swept the drugs they'd already rocked up inside the pillowcase, tied it up, and stashed it underneath the house, along with the gun he'd used to knock Trell down.

Hearing police car sirens closing in, Remo ran to the side of the house and peered around the corner. Red and blue lights shone on his face, as police cars stopped in front of the cookhouse.

Remo wasn't done yet. If he was going to sell the story he cooked up, he had to make it look believable, which meant he couldn't come out unscathed in this situation. He ran back inside the kitchen where he slammed his face into the kitchen counter twice, breaking his nose. Blood squirted and gushed out of his nose, and he staggered back, holding his hands over it.

"Aaaah, shiiiit. Fuck." Remo blinked back tears. He looked at his hands and they were bloody.

"Police! Open up," one of the cops announced, pounding at the front door.

Remo ignored the demands of the police, as he charged at the corner of the kitchen doorway. He slammed into it once and staggered backward, blinking his eyes. He charged at the doorway a second, and then a third time. Remo fell on the floor, with his forehead leaking, dazed and moaning. Staring up at the ceiling, he listened to the cop continue to pound at the front door and demand someone open it.

"Help. Help me. I'm, I'm hurt. My, my friend's been shot," Remo yelled, before everything went black. The last thing he heard was the cops kicking in the front door.

***

Remo assaulting himself left him with a total of twenty stitches in the forehead, splints for his swollen nose, and blackish-blue bruising around his eyes. To top it off, he had the granddaddy of all headaches, but he was hoping the Ibuprofen the nurse gave him would kick in soon. He was also dizzy. It wasn't from his charging at the doorway earlier, either. The blame fell on the shoulders of the two detectives that came asking him about what happened that night. They asked him the same series of questions, but in different ways. They were trying to trip him up, but he was too seasoned for that shit.

About forty minutes ago, Remo had hit up Wood to let him know what happened back at the cookhouse. Needless to say, he was hurt and angry at the same time. In Trell, he hadn't only lost a good soldier, but a god brother, as well. When Remo broke the news to him, he went silent, and for a moment, Remo thought he'd hung up. But then he heard him sobbing and breaking shit. The next thing Remo heard was his cellphone being handled like it was being picked up and placed to his ear.

"Remo, I needa know for sure that Trell's dead. I need you to tell me that you checked son's pulse and the whole shit," Wood's voice cracked emotionally. He went silent again, and Remo knew he was waiting impatiently for his reply.

"Yeah, bruh, they took 'em out. I'm sure of it," Remo assured him. "Them people came and zipped 'em up in that black bag."

Without saying a word, Wood hung up the phone and Remo's heart sank to his asshole. He didn't know what to expect, once he emerged from the hospital, but he knew he damn well had better be prepared for violence. He'd hid his gun underneath the cookhouse, so he didn't have it to defend himself.

After receiving his discharge paperwork, Remo got his prescription for Ibuprofen from the hospital's pharmacy. Walking toward the exit, he took out his cellphone to make reservations for a Lyft to pick him up. When he looked up, a black Suburban had just stopped in front of the emergency room's double door entrance. Its front passenger window descended and revealed one of many of Wood's soldiers, Hush.

Hush spat out Sunflower seed shells and addressed him. "What up, my nigga? Boss dawg wanna holla at chu." He poured some more seeds into his palm from the bag.

"Where is he?" Remo asked.

Hush tossed some of the seed back. "Inna back. Hop in."

Remo slipped his cellphone into his pocket, as he walked toward the Suburban. Discreetly, he took an ink pen out of his opposite pocket and slipped its cap off with his thumb. Though the ink pen wasn't as good as a gun, or even a knife, for that matter, it was better than nothing. Remo slid into the backseat and slammed the door.

Wood was sitting beside him, staring ahead, with dry tears on his cheeks. His eyes were glassy and pink, and he was clenching and unclenching his jaws. Remo took note of the machete lying on his lap and swallowed the lump of nervousness in his throat. He then zeroed in on the thick, pulsating vein in Wood's neck, and clutched his ink pen with deadly intent. He planned to strike that very vein, should Wood, or any of his goons, pose a threat to his life. "I've gotta dip out to drop this bad news on Trell's pops tomorrow, so I'ma need for you to tell me exactly what the fuck happened tonight," Wood said, looking at him like he'd bite his head off. "I don't want chu to leave not one, single, solitary detail out. I don't care if you stopped cookin' up the work to go take a shit. I want to know about it. Are we clear?"

"Yeah," Remo nodded understandingly. He then went on to tell Wood the same story he'd told him over the telephone, word for word. "The fools that hit the spot said they were only leavin' me alive to tell you that this was a Rich Loc block, and anyone lookin' to eat out here gotta cop their product from him."

"Rich Loc, huh? I've heard of 'em," Hush chimed in.

"Shit. Who hasn't?" Boodee said from behind the wheel.

"Nigga's crew strong and his money long, but I don't give a fuck," Wood voiced his thoughts. "I'll lock horns with the likes of Satan behind mine."

Wood sparked up a blunt and offered Remo a hit. The shit smelled a little off to Remo, and he started to decline it, but then he thought better of it. He knew how unpredictable Wood was, especially at that time. The mothafucka was liable to flip out and whack him in the backseat for refusing to get high with him.

Remo took the bleezy from between Wood's pinched fingers and took a few pulls from it. His eyes bulged as he coughed harshly and pounded his fist into his chest. Instantly, he started feeling funny, blinking his teary eyes, like he was cutting onions. Remo was so fucked up he didn't even notice Hush taking the blunt from him and indulging in it himself. Hush took a couple of drags before passing it to Boodee.

Remo looked at Wood, who was talking to his machete like it was his ride or die bitch.

"Yeah, shorty, we at these bitch niggas' throats that smoked my people. This shit here is personal, so I want you right by my side, when I hand down the penalty." Wood spoke softly to his machete, kissing it tenderly. For the first time, Remo noticed the name engraved on the side of the blade, LaCresha.

Remo's head was starting to hurt so he rubbed it. His eyes narrowed as he looked at Wood. "Yo, yo, yo, son, fuck kinda weed was that?"

"Wasn't just weed, my dude, it's that Woolah," Hush interjected, passing the blunt back to Wood. He smiled at Remo and then pointed out the location of where they were going to Boodee. "Right here, kid. You passin' the muthafucka up."

I can't believe this shit. These nut ass niggas got me smokin' weed mixed with crack. A muthafuckin' Woolah blunt, Remo thought, as he shook his head. He was feeling funny as shit and couldn't wait until his high came down.

Boodee busted a U-turn in the middle of the residential street and drove up behind Remo's whip. Remo hopped out of the truck, without saying a word. He started toward his ride, when the backseat window descended, and Wood's face emerged.

"Yo, Remo," Wood called after him. Remo turned around, wondering what his crazy ass wanted. "If it turns out you're lyin' about what happened at the cookhouse, I'ma tar and feather yo' ass. Word to Trell."

The Suburban drove away with the backseat window coming up and sealing Wood inside. Remo, who had his hand on the door handle of his car, stared at the backlights of the SUV, until it disappeared down the block. He took a scan of his surroundings to make sure there wasn't anyone watching him, and then he dashed to the back of the cookhouse. He recovered the pillowcase containing the drugs and the gun he'd used to murder Trell.

Slinging the pillowcase over his shoulder, he walked out of the backyard wearing a sly smile on his lips.

Yeah, nigga, this shit comin' together like butt cheeks. Inna minute, I'm bouta be top dawg out this bitch.

Chapter 16

Biggie zipped through the streets in Rich Loc's royal blue Lambo, disturbing discarded trash on the pavement. His mind journeyed back to something Golden told him about the assets they'd stolen from Rich Loc.

Golden frowned as he looked at Rich Loc's chain, which was hanging around Biggie's neck. He had its icy-gold piece pinched between his fingers. "Yo, whenever you fence this shit and the Lambo, make sure you do it far from home. We don't want what we did tonight coming back to bite us in the ass."

Biggie nodded. "A'ight."

Golden placed his hands on his shoulders and looked him in the eyes. "Nah, you're not hearin' me. I'm serious, bruh. You fence this shit outside the city line. Comprende?"

"I said, 'a'ight', Golden. Damn."

"I'm not goin' way out to the next borough to pitch this muthafucka," Biggie thought aloud. "I'll just threaten homie to keep shit onna low, or I'll see to it he eats a box of bullets." He turned the volume up on Future's "Like That" and punched out, breezing through an intersection.

Baby Girl, in her booger green and black Dodge Challenger SRT, swept through the intersection's traffic light, as it turned red, gaining on her twin's trail.

***

Coley sat behind the desk in his office, throwing darts at a board hanging on the wall. Coley was a tall, slender brother, with a bald head and goatee. Six days a week, one could find Coley at his business, rocking the same denim jumpsuit he always had. The man didn't look like much, and he didn't put much into his appearance. His only concern was making money to support his family, which was why he kept long hours and dealt with some of the city's shadiest characters. Street niggas knew they could come to Coley for the disposal of a body, or cash in on stolen luxury vehicles. He had a hand in most of the city's illegal proceedings, whether it was transporting dope, or human trafficking. If it could turn a decent profit, then he wanted in on it.

Coley threw the last dart, and it struck the bull's-eye of the board. He chucked what was left of his turkey sub in his mouth and snatched the napkin from his collar. He balled up the napkin and shot it across the room toward the wastebasket.

"LeBron," Coley called out. The balled-up napkin deflected off the side of the wastebasket and landed on the floor.

He picked up the can of Pepsi and washed his sandwich down. Belching, he shot the can directly into the wastebasket. Hearing knocking at his office door, Coley got up and peered through the blinds. He saw his guy, Harry, flanked by Biggie and Baby Girl. A smile graced Coley's lips when he saw Biggie. He knew whenever that nigga came through, he had a joint he could make mad money off. On top of that, he had Baby Girl's fine ass with him. He'd tried to get at her on several occasions, but shorty never had any holler for him. That didn't stop him from trying, though. The way he saw it, she'd eventually fall for a Get Money Nigga like him. Money was like Kryptonite to young, badass; hood bitches like her. Luckily for him, he had plenty of it.

"Who is it?" he called out.

"Amari," the voice replied from the other side of the door.

"What is it that you want, Amari?"

"I've got some business I'd like to discuss."

"Gimme a sec," Coley replied, hustling back to his desk.

He pulled open the top drawer and retrieved a bottle of Cool Water cologne. He dabbed a little into his palm, smacked his hands together, and slapped it upon his neck and chest. Coley then snagged a bottle of Binaca and gave his mouth and tongue two good sprays. Afterward, he dropped the bottle back in the drawer and pushed it closed. He cleared his throat and brushed imaginary lint from his chest and arms, before proceeding towards the door. Coley opened the door and stepped aside, trying his best to look cool.

***

Wood's black Suburban navigated its way through the labyrinth of alleys and boulevards that made up the concrete jungle he called home. Wood stared out of the back passenger window through black sunglasses. His mind was plagued with memories of him and Trell. He didn't know it, but a smirk formed on his lips. Boodee glanced up at the rearview mirror and thought he was tripping when he saw it. He found it odd that his boss had a smirk etched across his face. He'd been a depressed, raving maniac since the news of Trell's death hit.

"Yo, Wood, it's comin' up, pass me yo' piece," Hush told him. "You, too, nigga," he addressed Boodee.

"My shit is under my seat," Boodee replied.

"Well, grab it, B. I'm not reachin' between yo' legs," Hush said.

Once Hush had Wood and Boodee's guns, he placed them inside of a secret compartment that one would have to have X-ray vision to locate.

Wood sat up and looked through the windshield at the imposing structure of the federal penitentiary. It was guarded by impressive watchtowers and floodlights. Wood prepared himself as best as he could for the task ahead. His mind was racing crazily, and his shoulders were heavy with the burden of reporting the tragic death of a loved one.

Once Boodee drove through the barbed wire gates of the corrections facility, two corrections officers emerged to examine the Suburban, to make sure they weren't bringing any contraband on the premises. After the truck had been thoroughly examined, everyone was searched, and then Boodee was shown where he could park.

Wood made his way across the parking lot, smoothing out the wrinkles in his clothes, and taking in his surroundings. Although he was knee-deep in the trenches, he wasn't your average street nigga. He operated by a code—a code of loyalty and respect. Right now, he was about to honor that code by delivering some devastating news to Trell's father, Chaka, who was serving time behind bars.

Wood entered the facility, acknowledging the guards with nods, as he passed through security, metal detectors humming, as he stepped through them. Inside the visiting room, he spotted Trell's old man, sitting alone at a worn-out table. His face was weathered, and his hands were calloused from years of hard living. Wood approached cautiously; the gravity of his mission weighed heavily on him.

Chaka rose from his chair and walked around the table to greet his godson. Wood took notice of his appearance. He'd packed on the pounds, since he'd been down. He had a big pie face, a protruding belly, and fingers the size of Polish sausages. He had a five o'clock shadow and the hair of his crown was noticeably thinning.

Chaka smiled as he opened his arms for a hug. Wood gave him a weak smirk in return. It was the best he could do, considering the circumstances.

"It's good to see you, son. How have you been?" Chaka asked, sitting back down at the table.

"I'm coolin, unc," Wood replied, trying his best to avoid eye contact.

Chaka looked at Wood through narrowed eyes. He could tell something was wrong from his demeanor "What's going on, Woody?" He addressed him by his childhood nickname. His father had given it to him on the account he was crazy about Woody Wood Pecker as a child.

Wood took a deep breath, steeling himself for what was to come. "It's about Trell, Uncle C," he began, his voice steady, despite the knot tightening in his stomach.

Chaka's expression hardened, and a flash of concern crossed his face. "What about Trell? Spit it out, Woody."

Wood hesitated for a moment, searching for the right words. "He's, uh, he's, uh, gone, Uncle C," he finally managed to say, the weight of his words hanging in the air like a basketball player after a slam dunk.

Chaka's eyes glazed over and he looked away, sliding his hand down his face. He then looked back at Wood and asked him what happened. Wood took a deep breath, and his shoulders slumped. He recounted the same story Remo told him.

"Rich Loc, huh? I know exactly who that is," Chaka said.

Before he could say another word, Wood beat him to the punch. "Uncle C, I swear on my father's grave, the muthafucka that hit Trell is gon' get his. My word is bond." He gave him a dead serious look, as tears slid down his cheeks unevenly.

"I'm gonna hold you to that, son."

"I wouldn't have it any other way."

Wood bought Chaka a few things from the vending machine. He listened to the penitentiary gangsta as he recounted street tales about him and his father's felonious capers. Wood loved hearing about how his old man used to put it down in the streets. It made his heart swell with pride and fueled him to lay down his gangsta.

The downside of Wood hearing about his pop's exploits was his feeling depressed afterward, and missing him terribly. Wood's father, Dibbz, and Chaka made the mistake of jacking a truck carrying a precious load. They thought they'd come up on some flat-screen televisions, but they winded up with two hundred bricks of raw. They knew they couldn't return the product, and even if they could, there wasn't any way that they would. They were jack boys, and jack boys never gave back what they took.

When word got around some niggas out of Brooklyn were trying to get off a few birds, the cartel that the drugs belonged to rolled into town. They kidnapped Dibbz and tortured him for the whereabouts of their merchandise and his partner in crime. Dibbz held it down like a G. He didn't tell the cartel shit, so they chopped off his head and mailed it to his mother's crib. It was Wood that signed for the package and opened it. What he saw inside gave him a serious mind fuck and left him dependent on psych meds.

"Alright, people, the visiting hour is officially over. Say your goodbyes and leave through the way you came in," a corrections officer announced over the loudspeaker of the visiting room.

Wood and Chaka got up from the table and hugged. Chaka cupped his face and looked into his eyes. "Remember, you gave me your word, Woody."

"And my word is bond."

Wood wanted to say something that would comfort Chaka, but he knew there weren't any words that could ease the burden of the grief he carried now. He understood that in times like these, true strength wasn't measured by the absence of pain, but by the courage to face it head-on.

Wood watched as Chaka and the other inmates headed back to their cell block. Chaka walked with a noticeable bop that most onlookers mistook for swagger, but there were those, like Wood, that knew better.

With Dibbz gone, Chaka was left with the task of selling the kilos. He found a buyer, and they agreed to link up at an old, abandoned gas station. It was just too bad for Chaka that the nigga he was selling the work to was an undercover cop. He couldn't see himself spending the rest of his life in the feds, so he held court in the streets. He ended up on the losing end of that gun battle, with a bullet in his stomach and another one in his kneecap. He was eventually hit with a life sentence and shipped off to begin his bid.

Chaka's troubles on the outside of the walls followed him inside. The cartel sent two Mexican gangbangers to assassinate him. He surprised the hell out of them, putting one in intensive care and putting the other in the morgue.

Wood gathered with the other visitors to walk out of the prison. He didn't know how he was going to do it, but he was going to find Rich Loc, and make him pay for what he had done to Trell.

Chapter 17

"The Lamborghini Sián. Only sixty-three of these beauts were made," Coley said, taking a good look at the car, as he walked around it. "Did you know these babies go for 3.6 million a pop?"

Biggie and Baby Girl whistled and exchanged glances, hearing how much the Lamborghini was worth.

"You interested in buyin' it?" Biggie asked.

"Hell yeah," Coley replied, kneeling to take a good look at the tires.

"Look, I'm notta greedy man, so let's say you slide me, uh, two out the doe," Biggie said.

Coley walked around to the back of the Lamborghini. His brows wrinkled when he saw its plates, *RICH*. He threw up a grin and nodded to the bread Biggie wanted for the sports car.

"You've got yourself a deal, my man," Coley shook Biggie's hand. Biggie couldn't stop smiling. "You've gotta gimme a minute, though. I don't have that kinda loot lyin' around the shop, so let me make a call. You all sit tight."

Coley stopped grinning once he'd walked away from the twins. He locked his office door behind him, drew the blinds closed, and picked his cellphone up from his desk. With one hand on his hip, he paced the floor, listening to the telephone ring.

"Yo, Rich, get cho ass down to the shop, pronto," Coley told Rich Loc, before taking a peek through the blinds. He could see the twins sitting on a bench by the restrooms, chopping it up. "I've got yo' Lamborghini sittin' here at my spot, and with the two muthafuckaz that stole it, too. You're gonna owe me big time for this one, nigga." He cracked a grin.

Coley disconnected the call and slipped his cellphone inside his pocket. He took the time to put a smile on his face before opening his office door.

"How would y'all like somethin' to drink, while we wait on yo' money?" Coley asked the twins, as he shut his office door behind him.

***

"Keep 'em there, Coley. You keep 'em there, and you can keep my Lambo, plus I'll throw in a bag for yo' trouble." Rich Loc hung up his cellphone and pocketed it. He ran his naked ass around to the other side of the bed, dick swinging.

Aries frowned as she stood up, wiping her mouth. She was in the middle of sucking Rich Loc's dick, when Coley called him. "What's the matter? What's going on?"

Rich Loc buckled his belt and slipped his shirt over his head. "That nigga, Coley, found my Lambo, and he has the cocksuckaz there that stole it."

Aries went to say something, but winded up getting glassy-eyed and choked up. She feared Golden was the poor soul who was unknowingly waiting to be chopped down by Rich Loc and his goons' AK-47s.

"Who, who was it that stole yo' car?" Aries asked.

Oh, God, please, don't let 'em say Golden. Please, don't let 'em say Golden.

95

"I don't know, but I will when I get there," Rich Loc said, turning around from his opened closet with an AK-47 and cocking it.

"I'ma come with you." Aries slipped on her panties and bra.

"Nah, boo, you sit this one out. I'ma handle these hoes for the both of us." He kissed her on the cheek, as he walked toward the door on his cellphone. "Parelli, what's up, gang? Yo, I need you to round up the guys and meet me over at Coley's. Found the niggas that stole my ride."

Aries listened closely for the front door to close, before racing into the living room. She stole a peek through the blinds and saw Rich Loc backing out of the driveway and speeding away. She ran back inside his bedroom, grabbed her cellular, and plopped down on the bed. She speed-dialed Golden and waited impatiently as his phone rang. When he didn't answer, she called him again and again, until he finally picked up.

"What's up, lil mama?" Golden said.

Aries sobbed uncontrollably, with teardrops falling from her eyes. Hearing her sobs, Golden feared for the worse. She couldn't see him, but she knew he'd loaded up his gun and cocked it. She could hear him doing it.

"Yo, what the fuck is goin' on? That bitch ass nigga do something to you?" Golden asked. He was running out of the house and to his car.

"No. I'm just so, I'm just so glad you're alive."

"Huh? Why wouldn't I be alive?"

"Rich Loc gotta call from his mechanic, Coley. He said he has his Lambo at his shop, and the niggas that stole it," Aries informed him, and then blew her snotty nose. "I thought it was you, babe. I thought it was you," she broke down sobbing again.

"Shit. He hadda been talkin' about the twins. That's who went to fence the Lamb today," Golden said. "Yo, I've gotta make it up there to them before yo' punk ass fiancé does. Gimme the addy." Aries gave him the address and he hung up, without saying bye. He then called his mother. "Yo, ma, shit is about to hit the fan. This is code red. I need you to link up with me at this address. You gotta pen?"

***

Jynx lay stretched across the couch with a pit-bull puppy in his lap, watching television and sharing a blunt with Parelli.

Rich Loc had given Jynx time off with pay, since he'd gotten wounded during his encounter with Cowboy. Since he'd been released from the hospital, the young street soldier had been spending his days smoking weed, watching T.V., and tending to his pups. He looked at his down time as a vacation, and though he was enjoying it, he couldn't wait to get back to work.

Jynx was a street nigga and he loved being in them. He felt like a duck out of water, when he couldn't be out on the land with his locs, in the mix of things. Yesterday he'd started to hit up Rich Loc and tell him he was ready to get back to earning his keep, but the pain from his wound had him bawling like a baby. The Tramadol the doctor prescribed wasn't doing anything for him, but the cocaine seemed to bring him instant relief. At first, he only indulged in it when he was hurting, but that gradually turned into him using it recreationally. He tried to fight the urge to use it, but it's calling of him became too loud to ignore, and he'd have to feed the monkey on his back.

Jynx knew without a doubt he'd gotten himself hooked on coke and regretfully became what he vowed he'd never be, an addict, just like his old man. He promised himself that once his wound healed, he was going to shake his habit and only smoke weed.

Although Jynx was blowing trees right now, he was dying to toot some powder. The only thing standing between him pampering his nose was Parelli. As quiet as it was kept, Jynx looked up to Parelli, and he wasn't too fond of fiends. So, he was sure if he found out that he was playing with his nose, he'd shun him and lose all respect for him. That was something Jynx wasn't sure he was ready to deal with yet.

"Yo, those full-blooded pits you're raisin' back there?" Parelli asked from the opposite couch.

"Yep," Jynx replied, passing the blunt back to him.

"Son, you got like, what, twelve, thirteen pups?"

"Something like that." Jynx rubbed his pup and kissed him.

"You ever thank about sellin' 'nem? You could make a fortune."

"I know. I've been thinkin' about leavin' these streets alone and takin' up breedin' full time."

"That's a smart move. Well, shit, if you ever lookin' for a part…" Parelli stopped short on account of his cellphone ringing. "Hold up, son, this my shorty. What up?" Parelli answered the call. He frowned and sat up, having been told something serious. "What? What hospital are you at? A'ight, I'll be up there in a hot minute. I love you, too." He disconnected the call.

"What's hap'nin', kid?" Jynx looked at him with concern.

"Kaylonni dizzy ass hadda car accident." Parelli tucked his gun as he rose from the couch. "She sounded real fucked up, too, son. I'm finna roll up there to see what the deal is." He shook up with Jynx as his cellular rang again. "This is probably her again." He looked at his cellphone's display. "This that nigga Rich. Lemme see what's up with my loc."

Parelli answered the call, walking around the living room and listening to what he was being told.

Jynx watched him as he continued to stroke his pup. He didn't know what was up, but he gathered it was something serious from the look on Parelli's face.

"Yo, you know any other time I'd come runnin' to tear shit up with the gang, but my shorty got into a real bad accident." Parelli listened to what he was being said before replying. "Nah. I'm here at cha boy, Jynx's crib."

Jynx sat up on the couch and threw his head back like, *what's up?*

"Aye, hold on." Parelli held his cellular to his chest so Rich Loc wouldn't overhear him. "Rich said a couple of the fools that jacked 'em are at Coley's shop, tryna slang his ride to 'em. He's callin' for all hands on deck to get with these dudes."

Jynx thought about what he had been told for a moment. "Yo, son, if you can't roll, tell 'em I'm game," Jynx told him. He was dying to get in on the action. He'd been laid up at the crib since he'd caught a hot one, and boredom was pushing him to the edge of his sanity.

Parelli stared at Jynx for a minute, trying to decide whether he should protest his request to roll out with the kill squad. He knew Jynx was a street nigga, like himself, so he lived to be in the mix. He craved action, like a vampire craved a taste for blood.

Fuck it. This nigga grown, Parelli thought, before getting back on the jack with Rich Loc. He told him he couldn't come along on the mission to get his whip back, but Jynx was down to ride.

Jynx's eyes were full of hope that Rich Loc would agree to let him link with the kill squad to get back at his assailants. Parelli couldn't see it, but he had his fingers crossed.

"I'll let the homie know what's up. A'ight, my G, peace." Parelli hung up with Rich Loc and hollered at Jynx. "You're on, loc. The homies gon' scoop you up in like twenty minutes."

"Good lookin' out, son," Jynx said, dapping him up and giving him a thug hug.

Parelli tried to pass Jynx what was left of the blunt they'd been sharing, but he declined his offer.

Jynx locked the door behind Parelli and placed his pup back inside the kennel with the other pit-bull puppies. He retreated to his house, where he got dressed in his killer shit and waited on the front porch for his ride.

As soon as Jynx's ride rolled up, he hustled down the steps and hopped into the backseat. The backdoor slammed shut and the car drove off.

Chapter 17

Rich Loc, in his royal blue '96 Chevy Caprice Classic, flew up the street, with three hoopties full of his goons trailing behind him. Their thoughts were on the mission at hand, as they cocked their choppas.

***

Shirvetta stuck her automatic pistols inside her shoulder holsters and snatched her trench coat from the coat stand. She ran out of the house, slipping it on. She jumped inside her whip and zoomed out of her driveway in reverse. Throwing her car back in drive, she floored the pedal and zipped up the block.

Code red meant that a family member or members were in grave danger, and everyone was needed, as soon as possible.

***

Seeing he was nearing the address, Golden pulled out his gun and laid it on his lap. He picked up his cellphone and tried calling Biggie for the fifth time, but again, he was sent straight to voicemail.

"What the fuck is up with this lil nigga's phone, bro?" Golden's brows wrinkled as he looked at the screen of his cell.

***

Rich Loc's Chevy was the first to drive into the parking lot of Coley's shop, followed by the whips of the rest of his goons. Rich Loc emerged from his whip, blowing smoke out of his mouth and flicking what was left of a blunt aside. His goons hopped out of their cars behind him, wearing blue bandanas over the lower half of their faces. Rich Loc pulled a blue Pooh Shiesty mask over his face and charged toward Coley's shop, motioning for Locs to follow him.

***

Coley was reciting a bunch of corny ass jokes, and the twins were exaggerating their laughter, for fear of losing the sale of Rich Loc's Lamborghini. The laughter died down when Biggie's cellphone rang.

"Hold up, son. This my bro." Biggie placed his cellphone to his ear. "What up, big bruh?"

Coley was looking Biggie dead in his eyes as he talked on the phone. He watched as the jovial expression vanished from his face and a scowl formed. The young nigga looked up at him with hatred in his eyes and his nostrils flared. Right then, he knew his brother had just revealed the setup to him. Before his brain could communicate to his legs to run, it was entirely too late. Biggie drew his tool and popped him in the forehead. Coley's head flew backwards and chunks of brain went with it. Baby Girl looked shocked to see what her brother had done in front of her.

"What the fuck, Biggie? What chu do that for?" Baby Girl shouted angrily.

"It's a setup," Biggie told her. The side door of the garage opened and one of Rich Loc's goons charged through it.

Biggie shoved his twin aside and sent a bullet at him. The bullet zipped through the goon's heart and he fell awkwardly to the ground. Baby Girl, seeing the mechanics come from under the hoods of cars and toolboxes with guns, pulled out her own and started laying fools down. Body after body met with the pavement and spilled blood.

Boom!

Shirvetta kicked open the door on the opposite side of the garage. She ran inside, pistols up, shooting at anyone that she didn't push out of her womb. Golden came in behind her, bandana over the lower half of his face, doming niggas, knocking them off their feet. Bullets were flying back and forth on both sides. Shattered glass and shrapnel flew everywhere. Niggas screamed and hollered as hot bullets seared through the fabric of their clothing and melted into their skin.

"Gaaaah!"

"Aaaaaah!"

"Graaaah!"

While the gun battle raged, Rich Loc hunched down with his AK-47 and hurried over to a box Chevy. Placing his choppa down on the driver's seat, he pushed the hood classic in Golden's direction. He grabbed his AK off of the driver's seat as the vehicle picked up speed, flying in its intended target's direction. Golden was so busy taking shots at everyone coming for his head that he neglected to watch his back.

"Oh, my God, Golden, watch out," Shirvetta yelled across the garage, tackling her second oldest son to the ground, and sending his gun sliding underneath one of many cars.

"Fuckin' bitch," Rich Loc said under his breath, pissed Shirvetta had gotten in the way of his killing her son. He ran up on the roof of a Tesla, spraying his assault rifle like a lunatic. Golden, having seen him running up on the electric car's roof, grabbed his mother and turned over with her in his arms. Her face balled up and she clenched her teeth, feeling a burning sensation rip through her left thigh and bicep.

Oh, yeah, I got these muthafuckaz now, cuz. I got 'em, Rich Loc smiled wickedly behind his Pooh Shiesty mask, as he quickly reloaded his assault rifle. He jumped down to the hood of the Tesla, and then to the pavement. He walked up on Golden and Shirvetta, to finish them off. Golden, acting as a human shield, placed himself between Rich Loc's choppa and his bleeding mother, fully prepared to sacrifice his life for hers.

Rich Loc pinned his AK-47 on Golden and... *Boc, boc, boc, boc, bloc, bloc, bloc, bloc*! He did a funny little dance as Baby Girl and Biggie ran up to him, blasting. He fell to the pavement and lost his choppa. He pulled a Desert Eagle from the holster at the small of his back and started busting at the twins.

Catching hell from Rich Loc and his goons from two directions, Baby Girl and Biggie ran to take cover. Baby Girl sought shelter first, while Biggie laid down cover fire for her. Once he saw Golden had pulled Shirvetta to safety, he joined Baby Girl and reloaded his gun.

Bullets flew all around Baby Girl and Biggie, while they stayed on their bended knees, waiting for their chance to give a proper response. Once the fire ceased, Baby Girl and Biggie listened to the goons reload their assault rifles. Biggie, eager to knock down their opps, turned around to take a shot and a bullet sparked off the side of the vehicle he'd taken cover behind. In what seemed like slow motion, shrapnel flew at him like an object in a 3D movie.

"Aaaaaaaaah," Biggie hollered in agony, as the shrapnel sunk into his left eye. He fell to the ground and dropped his piece. Seeing her brother was out of the battle, Baby Girl picked up his gun and continued the firefight.

While all of this was going on, Golden had removed his belt and tied it around his mother's thigh to slow her bleeding. He then swiftly removed her belt and tightened it around her arm, to slow the bleeding there, also.

"I'll be okay, Golden. Go, go help your, your sister," Shirvetta strained, squaring her jaws, fighting back her aching wounds.

"A'ight, momma, sit tight. I'ma see to it you get outta here," Golden kissed his mother's forehead and scanned the ground for her guns. He found one, checked its clip, and popped it back in. Hunching over, he hurried over to Biggie, who was sitting up against an all-white '64 Chevy Impala on gold 100-spoke wire rims. "Lemme take a look at that eye, Big."

Golden held Biggie by the lower half of his face and took a good look at his wound.

Biggie growled low, trying his best to fight the pain. "Fuuuuck, bruh. This shit hurts."

Golden sat his gun on the ground and focused his attention on Biggie's wound. "Hold still, baby bruh, I'm tryna get this piece of metal outta ya eye."

Golden pulled the shrapnel out of Biggie's face and tossed it aside. He then picked up his gun and placed it in Biggie's hand. "Take ma and get the fuck outta here. You got it?" he asked, closing Biggie's hand around the gun.

"Yeah. I got this," Biggie assured, nodding. He dapped up with Golden and gave him a brotherly hug. At that moment, the beef they had was dead. It was family above everything else.

Golden picked up two guns, lying among the dead bodies of the mechanics they'd laid down. He and Biggie exchanged nods. Golden crept up beside Baby Girl as she was reloading her sticks. He started popping off, to give her time to finish reloading.

Biggie pulled Shirvetta's arm around his shoulders and helped her walk toward the backdoor. He turned around occasionally and sent heat at the warring fraction.

Police car sirens were wailing loud and furiously, quickly closing in on the location. Rich Loc sat up against the side of a silver BMW 745Li, gritting as he felt underneath his bulletproof vest. One of the slugs that hit him made it through his body armor.

"Awww, fuck, cuz. Sssss," Rich Loc ground his teeth, as he worked the bullet out of his pectoral muscle. Flinging the bullet aside, he looked to where he'd crawled from and saw a trail of blood drops. He pulled out his cellular and hit up his connect in the police department. "I'm in a bad way, my nig, I need you A-S-A-fuckin'-P. I know you hear that noise, yo' folks closin' in, and I'm sho' next gon' be the ghetto bird. Meet me at…"

Rich Loc gave his connect the location to meet him, hung up, and got up on his feet. Using the butt of his Desert Eagle, he broke the BMW's driver-side window and hotwired it, like a seasoned car thief. As soon as it turned on, he tied its wires together and got into the driver's seat. He mashed the gas pedal, and the beamer took off. It built up speed, flying so fast past cars and everyone else that they looked like blurs. He tried to run down Baby Girl and Golden, but they dove out of the way. Lying on their stomachs, the brother and sister duo popped shots at the back of the BMW, shattering its back window and putting bullet holes in its bumper.

Rich Loc brought his head back up from ducking Baby Girl and Golden's relentless gunfire. The shutter of the garage was getting closer and closer to him. He was either going to have a wreck that would ultimately kill him, or he'd succeed in going through the shutter.

Rich Loc buckled his safety belt and put the pedal to the metal. "A'ight, here goes, here I come, muthafuckaz."

Bah-Boom!

Rich Loc blew through the garage, making sparks and shrapnel fly. The BMW crashed back to the ground and spun around. Rich Loc fled toward the chained gates of the shop, crossing paths with Biggie, who was headed back toward the garage. Rich Loc blew through the gates and knocked them down. He swung out into the street and zipped up the block. Right then, police cars flooded the grounds of the shop and cops hopped out. They drew their guns and took shelter behind their vehicles.

***

Baby Girl and Golden retreated toward Biggie's car, exchanging gunfire with what was left of Rich Loc's goons, until they were secure in the backseat. Biggie floored it and flew out of the opening in the shutter Golden created when he'd driven through it. The police helicopter flew over the shop as Biggie cleared its grounds.

Chapter 18

Jynx and the goons knew they were in a losing situation with the police surrounding the chop shop. Not one man among the lot could see himself shackled down on a bus headed to prison, though. They'd all rather go out in a blaze of hood glory, before allowing that to happen. So they prepared for the hour they were all sure would come sometime in the life they'd chosen.

Jynx removed a folded piece of aluminum foil from his back pocket. He opened it and revealed a white substance, cocaine. He tooted some of the powder up his nose and passed it to the goon beside him. The goon tooted some of the powder and passed it to the next goon, and he, in turn, passed it to the goon next to him. The aluminum foil made its rounds among the lot, until the coke was gone and everyone was as high as a kite.

The goons checked their assault rifles and prepared for one last "Hoo-rah." They sent a prayer up to the Big Man in the Sky then exchanged daps and/or hugs, before what was to be a lethal exchange.

***

The sun dipped low on the horizon, casting long shadows over the silent streets, and the scene outside of Coley's chop shop crackled with tension. Police cars lined the streets, their blue and red flashing lights reflected on surrounding buildings. The number of cops seemed to have doubled outside the shop. Most of them were wearing bulletproof vests, and those that weren't, were in full tactical gear. They'd all taken up positions behind parked vehicles and around corners, their assault rifles trained on the shady business, where Jynx and the goons were holed up.

Sergeant Nunez, a seasoned officer with years of experience under his belt, stood at the forefront, megaphone in hand, bulletproof vest strapped against his body. His voice boomed through the stillness, slicing through the tense air, like the blade of a katana.

"Attention inside. This is the police. You are surrounded. Come out with your hands up." Sergeant Nunez lowered his megaphone at his side and looked at his watch.

The Waiting Game had begun.

Back inside the chop shop, Jynx, with a grim determination, looked over his comrades. After a tense moment, he motioned one of them over, a twenty-year-old named Nico. Jynx draped his arm over the kid's shoulders and whispered in his ear what he wanted him to do. The young nigga nodded and wiped his snotty nose with the side of his hand. His nostrils had been oozing since he'd snorted the coke.

Nico tossed his assault rifle aside, pulled his blue bandana down around his neck, and threw up his hands. He approached the garage door and cracked it open.

"A'ight, we're comin' out, don't shoot," Nico called out with a shaky voice. Although he was high as shit, he was well aware of the serious situation he was involved in.

Sergeant Nunez watched with wary eyes as Nico emerged from the chop shop, with his hands raised in surrender. The sergeant signaled for his officers to hold their fire, and then motioned for one of them to move in to apprehend the young man.

"Get down on the ground. Hands behind your back," shouted the officer that Sergeant Nunez motioned to move in, his voice tense with authority.

Nico complied, dropping to his knees as the officer swiftly cuffed him and led him away from the tenement. But as he did, a sense of unease settled over Sergeant Nunez.

Wait a minute, something doesn't feel right here, Sergeant Nunez thought.

The tension in the air seemed to ease as the officers waited for the remaining armed men to follow suit. But to their surprise, when the remaining men emerged from the chop shop, they were all armed to the tee, holding AK-47s with menacing intent.

"Aaaaaaaaah," Jynx and the goons hollered, like soldiers charging into battle, as they ran out of Coley's shop. They sprayed their AK-47s and empty shell casings flew out of their weapons in blurs. Some of the cops screamed as they were riddled with bullets, taken by surprise by the abrupt attack.

Sergeant Nunez's heart sank as he realized the situation had taken a turn for the worse. He threw his megaphone aside, upped his M-16, and started blasting.

Ping, bing, ting, zing!

Holes rapidly appeared in Sergeant Nunez's unmarked Crown Victoria, as bullets from Jynx and the goons zipped dangerously close to him. The sergeant continued to open fire, as he retreated to the rear of his vehicle and took cover. He aimed his M-16 over the trunk of his car and sent heat in every direction the goons were coming from. The windows on the driver's side of his Crown Victoria shattered, and so did its back window. Nico threw himself on the backseats as the windows exploded and broken glass rained on him.

Meanwhile, Gunfire erupted from all directions as Sergeant Nunez's men and Jynx's goons unleashed a flurry of bullets on each other. The air filled with the overwhelming stench of gunpowder, blood, and the screams of the wounded, as both sides clashed in a deadly dance of violence.

Jynx and the goons were holding their own against the opposition's firepower. Though they'd lost three men on their side, they were proving to be a threat, with less than a handful of them. Jynx moved with the skill of a man with a decade of combat training, neutralizing cops and pushing forward to lay down the next.

Sergeant Nunez was doing the same on his end, when he laid eyes on Jynx. He knew he had to take him out, since he was the driving force of the kill squad. With his eyes on the prize, Sergeant Nunez crept toward Jynx, who was ignorant of his presence. He upped his M-16 to light that ass up like a Christmas night, when someone creeping at the corner of his eyes called for his attention. Sergeant Nunez swung his assault rifle around to the goon, chopping him down with ease. Before the goon's body could meet the ground, Sergeant Nunez swung back around to pop Jynx, but to his surprise, he was already gone. It was like he disappeared into thin air.

Ratatatatat!

Bullets ripped into Sergeant Nunez's back and came out of his front. His eyes bulged. He looked down at his bleeding wounds and vomited blood. Turning around, he saw Jynx with his smoking choppa pinned on him. Jynx gave him another burst of gunfire, causing him to fall dramatically against a police car and land on his back.

Sergeant Nunez blinked his eyes as tears rolled down the side of his face and blood ran out of the corner of his mouth. Time seemed to have slowed to a crawl to him. His senses reeled, and the world spun around him in a dizzying blur. His men shouted his name in alarm, their voices distant and muffled, like they were coming from underwater. Sergeant

Nunez tried to get up from the pavement, but his limbs felt heavy and unresponsive. It was like they were weighed down by an invisible force. Darkness began to creep at the edges of his vision, threatening to swallow him whole.

Sergeant Nunez lay motionless on the ground, his consciousness fading in and out as waves of agony washed over him. He tried to call out to his men, to rally them to his side, but his voice refused to cooperate. The firefight raged around him, a savage ballet of death and destruction. Bodies continued to fall on both sides, their lifeblood staining the pavement burgundy, as the conflict reached its brutal climax. And then, as suddenly as the battle had begun, it was over. The gunfire ceased and was replaced by an eerie silence, broken only by the groans of the wounded and the distant wail of sirens.

Sergeant Nunez struggled to lift his head, his vision swam as he surveyed the carnage surrounding him. Most of his men lay strewn on the ground. Their faces were pale and lifeless, and their uniforms were soaked in blood. Jynx's goons didn't fare any better. Their bodies were twisted and broken amidst the wreckage of their failed attack. With a heavy heart, Sergeant Nunez closed his eyes, as his strength faded with each passing moment. As darkness claimed him, once and for all, he whispered a silent prayer for his fallen comrades, and with that, he gave his last breath.

Seeing the police closing in on Coley's chop shop, Jynx and the remaining goon made a run for it, trading gunfire with the last surviving police officer. The last goon blew off the side of the police officer's head. The officer splattered the goon's face as he fell to his death. Jynx glanced back at his comrade and saw he was a bloody mess. He wanted to go back for him, but he knew he'd already expired, from the looks of him.

Police cars raced onto the grounds of the chop shop, flying past the dead bodies lying on the pavement. Determined to get away, Jynx ran toward the back of the shop, occasionally stopping to send a burst of fire at the law. The police helicopter's spotlight followed Jynx to the back of the shop. He ran right into a wall of police cars, and turned on his heels, retreating in the opposite direction. He slid to a stop when he saw the police cars that were already on him.

"Shit! I guess this is it, huh?" Jynx said to no one in particular. He turned around in circles, seeing he was surrounded. Right then, the pact he made with the goons inside the garage went through his mind. Then he saw a glimpse of the future. He was shackled down on a prison bus headed across town to the Belly of the Beast.

Nah. I'm not goin' out like that. They'll see me in a bag 'fore they see me inna cell. My word.

The police cars stopped, and all of the cops hopped out. Some of them had shotguns, while others had the gun they kept holstered on their hip. They took cover behind their vehicles, with thoughts of blowing Jynx away for what he'd done to their fellow officers.

"Throw down your weapon, place your hands on your head, and lie face down on the ground," one of the cops ordered Jynx.

Jynx smiled like he was taking his yearbook picture, turning his AK-47 around and pressing it against his chest. "Fuck y'all."

Blaaat!

Chunks of bloody meat and bone imploded from Jynx's back. He collided with the pavement and his choppa fell beside him. His eyes were bugged, and his lips were parted. The police helicopter's spotlight shone on him and gave him an eerie glow. The last thought that went through Jynx's mind was "I should have just stayed my black ass at home."

Chapter 19

Nico looked around at all of the chaos going on outside of the police car. If it wasn't for him witnessing it in the flesh, he would have sworn he was on a movie set. By the time the last shell casing fell to the ground, he understood that Jynx wasn't sacrificing him to the law, so he and the other goons could escape, he was putting him out of harm's way.

Nico scanned the bloody battlegrounds for signs of life, but he didn't see a soul moving among the lot. He figured now was his best chance of getting away, and he was going to seize the opportunity. Lying on his back, he kicked at the back passenger window again and again, creating a cobweb that expanded each time it was met with force. The vulnerable window met with another one of Nico's kicks and shattered. Using his sneaker, he swept away the shards of glass lining the window, so he wouldn't cut himself getting out.

Nico threw himself out the window but only managed to get halfway out. He wiggled around until he eventually dropped to the ground and knocked the wind out of himself. Wincing, he scrambled back up and took off running, avoiding the spotlight from the police helicopter. He ran into an alley in the middle of the block, placed his back against the piss-stained brick wall, and made sure there wasn't anyone looking for him. Once he figured he was alone, he popped his thumb out of place and slipped the handcuffs off his wrist. He then thanked God for allowing him to flee with his life and ran down the alley.

That night, Nico vowed to give up the criminal lifestyle and go legit.

***

Parelli turned off the television in the middle of a report about what happened at Coley's shop. He turned around to his baby mama, who was laid up in the hospital bed. Her head was wrapped in bandages, her arm was in a cast, and so was her left leg.

"What's the matter, baby?" Kaylonni's forehead wrinkled.

Parelli shook his head and walked over to the wall-to-wall window. He folded his arms across his chest and looked at the colorful lights of the city.

"Stupid. Stupid. Stupid. You stupid muthafucka," Parelli said under his breath, thinking of Jynx's decision to get in on the action at Coley's shop.

***

"Ain't this bouta bitch, cuz? This muthafucka ran outta gas," Rich Loc thought aloud, glancing at the gas meter. It was on *E*. The car shut off so he steered it towards the right side of a residential street and put it in park. He held his bulletproof vest up from his chest and looked at the gunshot wound in his pec. Hearing the laughter and shouting of children, Rich Loc looked through the windshield at kids driving around on mini motorbikes. He grabbed his pole from underneath the driver seat, as soon as the idea to rob one of their little asses formed in his head.

Rich Loc leaned against the whip he'd stolen from Coley's garage and scanned the area for any potential witnesses. He held his gun behind his back and casually strolled toward the little niggas on the mini motorbikes. The closer he drew to them, the louder and clearer their conversation became.

"Mannnn, I'd fuck the dog shit outta Mrs. Davis," one of the kids said, doing donuts in the middle of the street on his motorbike.

"Me too, gang, her yella ass thick as cold oatmeal," a second kid said, sitting on the seat of his motorbike. He was in the middle of trying to light up a cigarette.

"Now that's one thang me and this big head nigga can agree on," a third kid added, slapping hands and shaking up with the second one.

A fourth kid brought his motorbike to a stop, after zipping up the block. Squinting, he leaned forward, trying to get a good look at Rich Loc. The older man looked suspicious to him. He noticed he held one hand behind his back and kept looking around him. "Yo, who the fuck is this?"

Upon the fourth kid posing the question, the others turned in the direction that their friend was looking, but it was already too late. Rich Loc upped his pole on the kid sitting on the motorbike, taking pulls from a cigarette.

"Lil nigga get off yo' ride and on yo' stomach," Rich Loc spat. The youngster was moving too slow for him, so he kicked him off the motorbike. He fell on the pavement, wincing, with his burning cigarette beside him.

Rich Loc went to mount the mini bike when he caught one of the youths making a move. He clenched his jaws and swung his pole around at all of the minors. "Y'all lil muthafuckaz movin' around just a lil too much for me. You know what? All y'all young asses lay on the turf, like lil homie here," Rich Loc demanded, planting his sneaker on the back of the kid's neck he'd knocked off the mini motorbike.

All of the young niggas lay on their stomachs in the street. Scared, they prayed under their breath Rich Loc wouldn't hurt them. Rich Loc tucked his piece inside his waistband, revved up the miniature motorbike, and zipped up the residential block. The motorbike whined annoyingly, and his shirt ruffled against the wind.

***

Detective Rollins sat in his unmarked car, smoking crack. He took a long pull and blew smoke up at the ceiling. He laid his head back against the headrest and closed his eyes, taking the time to bask in the moment. He put the crack pipe to his lips and brought the flame of his lighter toward the end of it, when a knock at the driver's window startled him. The crooked detective dropped the crack pipe and reached for his holstered gun. He stopped short of grabbing his piece when he laid eyes on Rich Loc.

"Rich, you scared the livin' shit outta me," Detective Rollins said, touching his meaty hand to his chest. "Come around to the other side and hop in."

Rich Loc ran around to the other side of the Crown Victoria. As soon as he opened the door, he was pimp-slapped across the face with the overwhelming smell of singed crack cocaine. He scrunched his nose and turned his head, to avoid breathing the repugnant odor.

"Yo, son, let the windows down," Rich Loc told the detective.

"I'm onnit," Detective Rollins replied. After letting all the windows down, he picked up a bottle of cheap cologne and sprayed it around in his car. He then capped the bottle and motioned for Rich Loc to hop in.

When Rich Loc hopped into the passenger seat, the first thing the crooked detective noticed was his bleeding.

117

Rich Loc looked at the blood stain on his clothes that Detective Rollins was staring at. "I caught one back at the shop," he informed him, before going on to tell him what had occurred back at Coley's shop.

The detective tried to take a look at Rich Loc's wound. The dope boy protested, but eventually gave in to his request. His forehead wrinkled as he examined the gunshot wound. "It's not that bad, but you needa patch it up to slow the bleeding."

"Fuck that. A hospital is outta the question. Besides, the cops will come snoopin' around once they catch word my black ass is there," Rich Loc said. "You know how it goes when shooting victims check into the spital. They're required by law to reach out to the jakes."

"Right." Detective Rollins nodded understandingly. He looked at the crack pipe and the lighter in his hands and got an idea. He told Rich Loc what he had in mind to stop his bleeding. The dope boy thought about the detective's suggestion for a moment, before agreeing to go along with it. He pulled down the collar of his shirt and exposed his nasty wound.

Detective Rollins held the flame of his lighter to the end of his crack pipe until it glowed with an ember. He grasped Rich Loc's shoulder and brought the crack pipe to his wound. "Alright, kid, this is gonna hurt like a son of a bitch, so you may wanna brace yourself," he told Rich Loc.

Rich Loc clenched his teeth and looked away. Detective Rollins counted to three and pressed the crack pipe's ember into his wound. Rich Loc squeezed his eyes shut and bit down on his bottom lip, to keep from screaming, but the pain got the best of him.

"Aaaaaaaaah!" Rich Loc screamed, then bit down on his fist to stifle it.

Detective Rollins removed the crack pipe from Rich Loc's wound, and it had closed.

"That fuckin' shit hurt." He looked down at his gunshot wound.

"Yeah. But it's closed, though." He took another look at the dope boy's wound. "You probably need a little somethin' to dull the pain. Lemme help you out." He stuffed a couple more rocks inside of the crack pipe and held it out to Rich Loc.

"Man, I don't indulge in that bullshit." Rich Loc pushed the crack pipe out of his face.

Detective Rollins shrugged and took a few drags from the pipe.

Rich Loc looked at him with disgust and focused his attention out of the passenger window. He listened as police cars raced through the streets with their sirens wailing. He knew, without a doubt, they were headed to Coley's chop shop, and he was glad he'd cleared the area. He couldn't stop from wondering how Jynx and the goons made out, though.

***

Detective Rollins placed his crack pipe inside of the glove box and smacked it shut. He fired up his car, threw it into drive, and was about to drive off, when Rich Loc grabbed his arm.

"Hold up. What the fuck you doin'?" Rich Loc looked at him like he had a booger in his nose.

"What do mean what am I doin'? The heat has died down, and now I'm finna get the hell outta here."

"Man, you tryna get me caught up out here? I can't be seen witcho po-lice ass in the front seat of this car," Rich Loc told him. "Check it, slap them bracelets on a nigga, and put me in the backseat. I don't need niggaz thinkin' I'm workin' with nine. Dig me?"

"Relax, my friend, these windows are limousine tinted. You'd have to have X-ray vision to see through these bitches. Hop out and take a look."

Rich Loc got out of the car and walked around it, taking a good look at all of its tinted windows. The detective was right, but Rich Loc still didn't give a fuck. He wasn't taking any chances, so he had him cuff him and put him in the backseat.

Rich Loc had an elephant's shit load of things on his brain, so he used the time spent going to their destination to think and watch the streets out of the passenger window. He replayed the events that transpired back at Coley's shop in his mind and recalled the name one of the shooters called out before tackling one of her comrade's to the ground.

"Golden. That's what that muthafucka's name was. Golden." Rich Loc scowled as he recalled one of the shooters names.

Overhearing Rich Loc, Detective Rollins adjusted the rearview mirror and looked at him in the backseat. "What was that?" he asked.

"Golden. One of the muthafuckaz we hadda shootout with, back at Coley's, name was Golden," Rich Loc said. "He was down with the crew that jacked me and my girl, the night I told you about."

"Golden. Golden. Why does that name sound so familiar to me?" Detective Rollins asked no one in particular, turning the name over in his mind, over and over again. "I've got it. Golden Love. He's a part of the Love family."

"The Love family? I think I've heard of 'em. Aren't they a part of a mob that's known for juxin' niggaz?"

Detective Rollins nodded, and confirmed what Rich Loc had said. "That's them. There's five in their posse, six, if you include the father. He's inside on a murder beef."

"I'ma need you to get me everythang you can on the Loves. I don't give a shit how much it costs me, either. You just name yo' price."

"Okay then. I want half."

"Half of what? An ounce?" Rich Loc asked. When he didn't get a response, he threw out the next amount of dope he thought the detective would want. "Half a chicken?"

Detective Rollins nodded. "Straight drop. No cuts. I can cook it myself."

A half of a brick wasn't shit for Rich Loc to come off of, but he wasn't trying to let Detective Rollins know that. He believed, if he did, then he'd probably try to get more out of him. With that in mind, he pretended to think about his request for a while before answering.

"Okay. Half a key it is," Rich Loc said. Although he couldn't see the detective's face, he knew he was smiling like a sissy in a prison shower room.

"Deal. I'll have to swing by the office to get the files and then I'll drop you off wherever you want."

Rich Loc laid his head back against the seat and closed his eyes. He drifted off to sleep, but awoke to the driver's door slamming shut. Yawning, he looked out of the passenger window and saw Detective Rollins sit something on the roof of the car. He opened the backdoor and took him out of the backseat. Taking the handcuff key out of his pocket, he unlocked Rich Loc's metal bracelets and shoved what he'd sat on the roof into his chest. It was an attaché case.

"Everything you wanted to know about the Loves is in there. I made copies of all of their files," Detective Rollins told him. "Once you're done with those documents, do me a favor and burn 'em."

"I got chu. Word is bond," Rich Loc assured him and took in his surroundings. They were at the mouth of an alley, on a dark residential block. Half of the street lights were out, and those that weren't, were dim. So he was sure there wasn't anyone that could identify either of them.

"Now about that half a bird."

"Right. I'll hit cho line as soon as I get my hands on it."

"Cool."

Detective Rollins dapped up Rich Loc and drove down the alley. Rich Loc watched the backlights of his car, until they vanished down the trashy path. Walking down the street, he peered into the attaché case and saw his gun wedged inside with all the documents the detective made copies of.

Rich Loc entered the yard of an abandoned house, with boarded-up windows and dead grass littered with garbage. He sat on the stoop of the house, pulled out his cellphone, and ordered a Lyft to pick him up. Using the flashlight of his cellular, he began reading over the paperwork the detective had given him.

Chapter 20

Aries's heart raged war inside her chest when Rich Loc walked through the door. All of the blood staining his shirt gave her cause for concern because, if he came back hurt, it was possible Golden, or even someone in his family, was hurt, or even worse, dead.

"Oh, my God, baby, what happened to you?" Aries said, worry dripping from her words. She rushed to Rich Loc and took a good look at him.

He politely moved her aside and walked over to the dining room table. He sat down and opened the file Detective Rollins gave him.

"Do me a favor and make me a drink?"

"What would you like?"

"Something strong, real strong, so no chaser."

"Okay, baby." Aries walked toward the hallway, discreetly sending Golden a text.

Aries: *R u okay?*

"Aries," Aries froze. Her heart started beating fast again. Slowly, she turned around, fearing he'd ask who she was texting. "Grab the first aid kit. I'm gonna need you to clean this wound for me. Unh," he frowned, removing his shirt and revealing the bulletproof vest underneath it.

Aries walked down the hall and entered the bathroom, closing the door behind her. Feeling her phone chime with a text message, she looked at its display and saw Golden had sent her a correspondence.

Golden: *I'm straight. Why? What's up?*

Aries: *Our friend was hurt. It got me thinking about you.*

Aries got the yellow first aid kit from underneath the bathroom sink. She was about to walk out of the door when a thought came to mind. She lowered the volume on her cellular and slipped it into her back pocket. As she walked by Rich Loc, she glanced over his shoulder at the file he was looking over. She caught a glimpse of Golden's mugshot, as well as the rest of his family's criminal profiles. She swallowed the ball of fear that formed in her throat. She felt so sick to her stomach that she could have thrown up, but she kept it down.

"I'll be right back with your drink, babe," Aries told Rich Loc, as she placed the yellow first aid kit on the table top. Disappearing inside the kitchen, she placed her back against the wall and her hand over her chest. Her heart was beating like a Samoan on a drum, and she was weak in the knees.

Oh, God. Oh, my fuckin' God. He knows now. I've gotta tell Golden.

As soon as the thought entered Aries's brain, her cellular vibrated with another message from Golden, telling her what happened at Coley's shop.

Golden: *Yeah, I'm sure that shit is all over the news by now. You with that nigga?*

Aries: *Thank God you're okay. And yes.*

"Damn, ma, you makin' the liquor from scratch or somethin'?" Rich Loc called out from the dining room.

"My bad, love, I'm on it," Aries assured him. "Just feelin' a lil sick onna stomach."

Aries slipped the cellphone into her back pocket, loaded a glass with ice cubes, and poured Rich Loc some Louie XXIII. Scooping up the glass, she returned to the dining room to find him taking pictures of all of the Loves' mugshots.

"Here you go, Big Daddy." Aries handed Rich Loc his drink and kissed his cheek. She had him turn to the side in his chair, so she could clean his wound and bandage it. Opening the first aid kit, she kneeled in front of him, stealing a glance at Shirvetta's mugshot.

"Who is she?" her brows furrowed with fake curiosity.

"Queen Bitch of the crew that jacked us that night," Rich Loc informed, taking a sip of his drink. "When I left earlier, it was 'cause of a call I got from Coley. He had two of the fools up there, who had taken my ride. They were tryna slang that bitch to 'em…" Rich Loc went on to tell the same story that Golden told her, only it was from his perspective.

"How'd you get yo' hands on these documents?" Aries inquired, cleaning the dry blood around his gunshot wound.

"Detective Rollins, my connect at the police department," Rich Loc replied. "That reminds me. I need you to drop a package off to this nigga."

"What kinda package, sweetie?"

"Half a chicken."

"Damn."

"Please, that's peanuts to a boss. You know how a gangsta roll."

"Ol' arrogant ass," Aries smiled and shook her head.

Rich Loc took another sip of his drink. "Aye, it's the truth."

"Can't argue with that."

Feeling her cellphone vibrating in her back pocket, Aries finished dressing Rich Loc's wound and stood upright. "You know what, babe? I think I'll have a drink myself, and then when you're finished lookin' over those docs, you can massage yo' queen's feet." She smiled, boasting the deep dimples in her cheeks.

"I gotchu faded, shorty." Rich Loc grinned, as he studied the mugshot of Golden. He mad dogged the mugshot, like he was standing face to face with him. He wished he was, too, so he could blow his fucking face off.

Aries returned to the kitchen, grabbed a glass, and filled it with ice, once again. She stole a look over her shoulder, and Rich Loc was still looking over the documents in the file. Cautiously, she took out her cell and looked at its display. She had a text message from Golden. What he said nearly made her faint on the spot.

Golden: *Yo, if you really love a nigga, like you claim you do, you'd give my boy those red balloons, right now.*

Aries teared up and smacked her hand over her mouth. Her heart was beating faster now. She was stuck between a rock and a hard place.

Aries: *But I thought you wanted to give him the red balloons.*

Golden: *I did, but fuck it. Since you're there, I figure you can do it and save me a whole lot of trouble. Besides, I already gotta bring the cake and ice cream. It's the least you can do.*

Aries: *Okay.*

Aries wiped her eyes and took a quick scan of the kitchen. She zeroed in on the knife block on the counter. She glanced back at Rich Loc and he was still looking over the documents. Slipping her cellphone into her back pocket, she snatched a medium-sized steak knife from the block, and poured her glass halfway full of Louie. She held the steak knife behind her back as she left the kitchen, tears sliding down her cheeks. She crept upon Rich Loc with the stealth of a jaguar, and brought her deadly weapon from behind her back. Her hand trembled as she leaned toward him, unable to stop the tears from drenching her cheeks.

I'm so sorry, baby. I love you, Aries thought, as snot began to ooze out of her nose. The life they'd shared as well as the life they could have in the future zipped across her mind. She closed her eyes, clenched her jaws, and brought the steak knife into play. Rich Loc was so caught up in the documents that he'd become oblivious to the danger looming over his head.

Aries made an ugly face and her bottom lip shivered. This was it. She'd committed herself to the assignment that Golden had given her and she had to carry it out, or risk losing him forever.

"Oh, Jesus, I just can't…" Aries whined, dropping the steak knife and pinning it down with her foot. She wrapped her arms around Rich Loc's neck and accidentally spilled some of her drink.

A look of confusion crossed Rich Loc's face, as he wondered what was going on with his fiancée. He looked at her and grasped her arm. "What's the matter, ma? You just can't do what?" he asked with genuine concern.

"I was just thinking about what chu told me happened today, and I thought what if you never made it back to me? Christ, I don't know what I would doooo," Aries broke down sobbing, burying her face in the side of Rich Loc's neck. He held her arms and kissed her bicep.

"But I did make it back to you, and nothing can ever keep me away from you, queen," Rich Loc said sincerely. "Even if a nigga was to get wet up by one of these bitch ass niggaz out here, my love will be witchu forever. You're mine."

"Do you really mean that?" Aries asked, face soaking wet.

"That's onna set."

"Take me."

"Huh?"

"I want chu to fuck me, right here, and right now."

Rich Loc stared into Aries eyes and saw that she was serious as a heart attack. He turned around in his chair, grabbing her face and shoving his moist, warm tongue inside her mouth. They made out roughly, breathing hard through their noses, and getting undressed at the same time. Rich Loc kicked off his boxer briefs and jeans, leaving him in just his socks. Aries unclasped her bra and her breasts popped out, like duo airbags. She peeled her thong down her luscious thighs and slipped out of them.

Rich Loc licked her throat and gently bit around her neck, drawing a gasp from her lips. Using both hands, he caressed her perky tits and pulled on her nipples. Her clit became as hard as an elevator button and her twat oozed with moisture.

"Christ, this feels so goddamn good," Aries whined, licking her top row of teeth and biting down on her bottom lip.

As Rich Loc continued to work his magic, she tugged on his dick, and a clear gel seeped out of its pulsating head. He held a boob in each hand, closing his eyes and devouring them. Throwing her head back, she rubbed the back of his neck with one hand and his back with the other. Her mouth hung open. Her eyelids fluttered. The sound of him sucking on her breasts made her wet. She balled her toes and her pussy began to drip like a broken pipe.

Rich Loc led her over to the couch and leaned her over the back of it. He toyed with her nipples and kissed up her chest. He sucked on the soft flesh underneath her chin, making her whine and drip faster.

"I want chu. I want chu to make me feel good. I want chu all up in me," Aries said, rubbing her hands up and down his muscular back. "Fuck me, daddy. Give me some of that thug passion."

Rich Loc picked Aries up and sat her on the top of the couch. She started nibbling on his neck, and he hissed like a King Cobra snake. Licking the pads of his fingers, he rubbed his saliva on the head of his pole and stroked it passionately. Grasping Aries' neck, he leaned her back and rammed himself inside of her, down to his nut sack. He clenched her waist with his other hand, stared into her eyes, and began banging her like a maniac. Every one of his thrust made her body jerk and her hair bounce. Her eyes rolled to the back of her head. She groped her tits and manipulated her hard nipples.

"Aaaaaah! Yes. Oh, yes," Aries hollered as she was drilled.

Rich Loc stared at Aries' pleasured filled face as he smacked up against her, dropping a long dick inside of her, making her spray his trimmed pubic hairs. He rose to the tips of his toes, throwing pipe faster and faster. Veins bulge on his forehead and the rest of his body. Sweat slid down his face, dripped off the tip of his nose, and slid down his back. The more Aries hollered, the faster he went, chasing the nut he so desperately desired. Aries flickered her rigid love button. Her eyes turned over to their whites. Her mouth stretched so far open, Rich Loc could see the fillings in her back teeth.

"Aaaaaaah," Aries screamed loudly before her voice went out.

Using both hands, Rich Loc grabbed her neck and squeezed. Squaring his jaws, he scowled at her and pumped into her with a vengeance. She outstretched both of her, legs like a gymnast, and balled her toes. The veins in her face and neck became pronounced. She gagged and choked with a smile, begging him to squeeze her neck harder and harder. Saliva seeped out of the corner of her mouth and her face turned red.

"Unh, unh, unh," Rich Loc grunted louder and louder, blinking his eyes to stop sweat from getting into them. "Ah, shit. I'm finna bust. I'm finna bust," he announced, flaring his nostrils, and forehead wrinkling.

"Bust, ack, ack, bust all up in me. This, this pussy is yours, daddy."

"Aaaaaah, fuuuuck." Rich Loc burst deep inside of Aries, painting her internal walls. He shot up her club and the parking lot, then collapsed upon her. They flipped over on the couch and laid upside down on it.

Aries rubbed his back and kissed the top of his head. His heart was beating so fast he could hear it in his ears and she could feel it against her breasts. Aries moaned softly as she twitched from the orgasm she met right before he exploded inside of her womb.

"That was good, babe. That was really good," Aries smiled, staring up at the ceiling.

"Ummhmm," Rich Loc replied, with his eyes closed.

***

Aries, wearing a silk robe, made her way into the dining room. She picked up Rich Loc and her clothes and then the steak knife she nearly slit his throat with. She slipped the steak knife into the knife block and walked into the laundry room. After preparing the washer with everything she needed to wash the clothes, she took her cellphone from out of the back pocket of her jeans, and glanced over her shoulder to make sure Rich Loc wasn't behind her. Next, she shot Golden a quick text, letting him know she couldn't bring herself to kill Rich Loc.

Aries: *Again, I'm sorry, I couldn't find any red balloons. I hope you find it in your heart to forgive me.*

"What chu doin' in here?" Rich Loc spoke from behind Aries. She nearly jumped through the ceiling. She slyly slipped her cellphone inside of the pocket of her robe as she turned around to him.

"Babe, you almost gave me a heart attack. Jesus."

"My bad, boo." Rich Loc kissed her and wrapped his arms around her. "I was just wondering where you were. I got up to take a leak and you were gone."

"Well, I thought I'd get up and wash our clothes, as you can see." She turned around to the washer, closing its lid and turning it on.

"I meant to ask you if the cable guy came by to fix the internet service."

"Yeah. He came by," Aries replied, walking out of the laundry room with his hands latched around her waist. "He looked hood as a muthafucka, though, especially with those two tattoo tears at the corner of his left eye. Kinda looked like one of yo' guys."

"Hmmm. Now what the hell would one of my niggaz be doin' wit a square gig?" Rich Loc said. "Installin' cable boxes and internet ain't nearly enough loot for my locs."

"Yeah. That's what I figured."

Aries and Rich Loc disappeared down the hallway and into their bedroom.

Chapter 21

Bam, bam, bam, bam!

"Hold your fuckin' horses, I'm comin'," Dr. Abagnale called out, as he hurried down the stairs, slipping on his robe.

Bam, bam, bam, bam!

"I said, wait a minute goddamn it, I'm comin' for Christ's sake," Dr. Abagnale called out again. His voice was heavy and dripping with anger now. As he walked to the door, he slipped a .380 inside the pocket of his robe. Thanks to the handheld monitor that was linked to the surveillance cameras in and around his crib, he already knew who it was that had dropped by to see him.

Bam, bam, bam!

The harsh knocking stopped once the good doctor started unchaining and unlocking the front door. He snatched the door open and Golden and Biggie were standing before him. The brothers looked disheveled and worried, but the blood stains on their clothes was what gave the doctor cause for concern.

"What's the matter?" Dr. Abagnale asked, worried lines across his forehead.

"It's moms, man, she's been shot," Golden regretfully informed him.

***

Dr. Abagnale ran through the house flipping on light switches and opening doors. As fast as he was running, one would have thought he had a rabid dog on his heels, but that couldn't be further from the truth. Golden and Biggie were chasing after him, holding Shirvetta between them. Her eyes were narrowed into slits and her pupils were wandering around. She'd lost so much blood, she was on the verge of fading to black and knocking on Heaven's door.

Dr. Abagnale stopped at his basement door and placed his hand down on the screen of the digital identification scanner. The red light on the side of the door panel stayed red until he punched in a combination of numbers on the keypad. The light turned green and there was a metallic click. The door slid open, like the door of an elevator, and Dr. Abagnale ran down the steps. Golden and Biggie were on his heels, with a crying Baby Girl on their trail.

Dr. Abagnale directed Golden and Biggie to a gurney at the center of the floor, where they placed their mother. He pulled on a pair of latex gloves and grabbed a pair of scissors. He cut up the center of Shirvetta's shirt and cut up the leg of her jeans. Dr. Abagnale's eyes quickly assessed the severity of her condition, his mind racing through the steps needed to staunch the flow of blood and save her life. While Golden, Biggie, and Baby Girl stood aside, hoping for the best, Dr. Abagnale spoke to Shirvetta calmly and reassuringly, telling her exactly what he was about to do to help her.

"You hear me? Huh?" Dr. Abagnale asked, shining a light in each of Shirvetta's eyes.

"Ye-yes," Shirvetta replied weakly.

"Okay. Good," Dr. Abagnale said, clicking off the light and slipping it inside his pocket. From there on, the shady doctor's movements were precise and deliberate, as he worked to control his patient's bleeding and stabilize her condition. Every moment that passed felt like an eternity, the weight of responsibility was heavy on his shoulders, as he fought to stop the bleeding.

Sometime later, Dr. Abagnale turned around to Shirvetta's children and wiped the sweat from his brows

"Okay. I stopped the bleeding but she lost a lotta blood, so she's gonna need a transfusion," Dr. Abagnale informed Shirvetta's children. "What blood type are you, Shirvetta?"

"O-negative," Shirvetta replied weakly.

"O-negative. That's good, real good," Dr. Abagnale said, peeling off his bloody latex gloves and discarding them.

"Why is that good?" Golden inquired, with wrinkled brows.

"Well, O-negative is a universal blood type, which means anyone could be a match for her."

"Great. Well, where do you keep your blood packs stashed around here?" Biggie asked, looking around the basement.

"I have a lotta medical supplies, tools and some mo' shit, but unfortunately I don't have any plasma," Dr. Abagnale regretfully informed him. "That's a tall order."

"Wait. Biggie and I are O-negative, she can have some of our blood, right?" Baby Girl asked, with hopeful eyes. She was prepared to do whatever she had to in order to save her mother's life.

"I don't have that kinda equipment to perform a procedure like that," Dr. Abagnale said, pacing the floor and massaging his chin. He was giving something a serious thought.

"Fuuuck, son," Golden spat harshly, swinging at the air. He sat down in a chair and ran his hands down his face, taking a deep breath.

"Listen, I can get my hands on the equipment we'll need for the transfusion, as well as the blood," Dr. Abagnale told them, taking the time to clean the lens of his glasses.

"Lemme guess, it's gonna cost us mad coins to get it, though, right?" Biggie said, hanging his arm around his twin sister's neck.

"Nothin' in this world is free," Dr. Abagnale said.

"I don't give a shit what it costs, we're talkin' about ma's life here," Golden told Biggie. "Look, doc, get on the jack and holla at whomever you have to. I'll be back with a big bag."

"You got it," Dr. Abagnale replied, pulling out his burner cellphone and walking to the corner of the basement. He had a total of three cellular devices. One was for work, the second was for family, and the one he was using now was for his street clientele.

"Hello, Dandridge? Yeah. It's me. Listen, you still have merch? O-negative." Dr. Abagnale grinned and gave the twins a thumb's up. "Great. Take down my address."

***

A gray and black 1933 Cadillac 352 Town Sedan parked across the street from Dr. Abagnale's house. A six-foot-four man with milky white skin slid out of the driver's seat. His weathered face bore the marks of his countless years on this earth, each line and wrinkle telling a story of a lifetime lived. His stark white hair cascaded from underneath his hat and laid over the shoulders of his suit's jacket. He opened the backdoor of the sedan and a puny, five-foot-seven Black man, youthful in appearance, emerged with a bulky briefcase. He adjusted his oversized apple jack on his crown of curls and took in the suburban utopia. He plucked his right suspender like it was a string on a guitar and started in the direction of Dr. Abagnale's house. His chauffeur, the man with milky white skin, waited until he was let inside of the house before getting back behind the wheel of the Cadillac.

He took his cellphone from the recess of his suit's jacket and started scrolling through Instagram.

***

Baby Girl, pistol in her waistband, opened the front door wide enough for Dandridge to walk inside.

"Well, aren't chu gonna come in?" Baby Girl asked.

"Only if you invite me." Dandridge grinned.

Baby Girl frowned, thinking what he said was strange, but decided to play along. She couldn't afford to run him off, her mother needed his blood. "Please. Come in."

"I'm delighted to." Dandridge stepped inside the house.

Baby Girl locked the front door and exchanged introductions with Dandridge. She motioned for him to follow her inside of the kitchen. Upon entering, he saw his payment neatly stacked on the kitchen table.

"Is this for me?" Dandridge asked, peeling back half a layer of a stack and causing it to make a shuffling sound.

"Every last dollar, Mr. Dandridge," Baby Girl replied.

"Please, call me Deacon," Dandridge said, placing his bulky briefcase on the kitchen table and popping its locks. Inside were packs of blood nestled against each other. Their crimson hue was stark against the muted tones of their surroundings. Each pack represented a precious lifeline, a source of sustenance for those who walked the line between darkness and light.

Dandridge placed three blood packs on the kitchen table, closed his bulky briefcase, and locked it. He tucked his payment into both insides of his coat and extended his hand to Baby Girl.

"It was truly a pleasure to have met you," Dandridge smiled, displaying a mouth of iPod white teeth. He kissed Baby Girl's hand and bid her farewell, with a tilt of his apple jack. After she'd locked the door behind him, she looked through the living room window and watched him walk back to his car. She thought her eyes were playing tricks on her when he vanished into the air and then heard the car he was chauffeured in start-up to leave. Baby Girl blinked her eyes and ran her hand down her face. She figured she'd been up for so long she was seeing shit.

Baby Girl raced back inside the kitchen, grabbed the blood packs, and knocked on the basement door.

Ma, please pull through this. Please, she thought as Biggie opened the door and let her inside the basement.

***

Golden made his way back to the armory where he had a chunk of cash stashed. He tossed his bloody clothes in the washer, took a shower, and threw on a fresh fit. He grabbed a Macy's shopping bag and loaded it with dead faces. He wasn't sure of the amount the doctor wanted for his services, or how much the plasma dealer was looking for his merchandise, but he wanted to be sure he had enough.

Golden tucked his pole inside of his waistband and walked out of the bedroom. He stopped dead in his tracks when he saw a mysterious dark figure sitting on the couch. He couldn't make out who it was, but he knew it was a man from his silhouette. He had an AR-15 assault rifle lying on his lap, and it was pointed at Golden. The tension inside the living room was thicker than those bitches in Nelly's Tip Drill video. Golden didn't see how he was going to get out of this situation. With his back against the wall, he could only hope he was fast enough to draw his piece and take out homeboy perched on the couch.

"I know what you're thankin', big dawg, and I wouldn't do it, if I were you," the dark figure told him. "The odds are stacked too high against you. By the time you pull that stick halfway outta ya waistband, I'd have sliced you in half." He tapped the trigger of his assault rifle and a red dot appeared on Golden's chest.

Golden's forehead creased, and he looked down at the dot. He knew he didn't stand a chance against the assault rifle.

"Relax, dawg, I didn't come here to knock you down." He tapped the trigger of his weapon, and the red dot vanished. "I came here to have a civilized discussion, and hopefully leave here with a clear understandin' and a partnership."

"You wanna chop it up? We can chop it up, but first I needa know who the fuck you are?"

***

Golden stood on the opposite side of the living room listening to what the mysterious man had to say. He got an earful and then some. He was blown away when he found out the man was one of the goons with Wood, when he shot up his crib.

"This is yours, whether you choose to roll with a nigga are not," the mysterious man tossed a pillowcase at Golden's feet. He looked down at it and then back up at old boy. Reluctantly, he picked up the pillowcase and looked at its contents.

"What's this for?"

"The damage to yo' crib. I'm sure you can flip it and make a decent profit."

"No doubt."

The mysterious man got up from the couch with his assault rifle at his side. He walked up to Golden, and for the first time, he saw his face.

"So, what's up? You with the business, or what?" He extended his hand.

Golden looked at his hand for a while, before shaking it. "Yeah. I'm with it."

"Cool." The man held out his hand. Off top Golden knew he wanted his cellphone so he gave it to him. After programming his telephone number into it, he gave it back to him and walked toward the door.

Golden looked at the display of his cellular as the front door clicked shut. The name the mysterious man programmed his number under was Remo.

Chapter 22

Remo hopped into his whip and drove away from Golden's armory in the opposite direction he came. He adjusted his rearview mirror and took the time to light what was left of the blunt he'd been smoking earlier. Now that he had the Loves on his side, he was confident that he'd succeed in knocking Wood out of the way and taking his spot as top dawg. He'd already secured a plug on decent work, and once he took over all of Wood's traps and put his people in position, he could get the Money Ball rolling. He only had four niggas on deck that were down with his program, but he was sure, once Wood's soldiers were left starving after his demise, they'd come around begging to be down.

Remo knew he didn't have the manpower to go at Wood and his people, which was why he enlisted Golden and his tribe. The drugs he gave Golden were to let him know he was serious about working together and to get him to let his guard down. Once he saw an opening, it was lights out for the Loves, too. He couldn't leave any loose ends. The way he saw it, he would have to be a fool to trust a family of fucking thieves. Golden's people had a reputation for jacking drug dealers, and his goal was to be the biggest goddamn drug dealer in the city, so he'd be taking a chance allowing them to breathe.

"Look out world, ya boy's comin' for everythang I deserve, and then some," Remo thought aloud.

***

Golden was driving like the police were on his ass in a high-speed chase. He was concerned with his mother's condition and prayed that she was okay when he made it back. His cellphone started ringing, and his heart thudded when he saw it was Dr. Abagnale. He didn't know what he wanted, and truthfully, he was scared to answer his call to find out. Whatever it was he was hitting him up about, he knew he couldn't run from it. He'd have to man up and face it eventually, so he decided to open it.

Golden closed his eyes for a moment and mouthed a silent prayer. He then answered the call. It seemed like the doc was taking forever to say something, but he reasoned it was his paranoia that had him jacked up mentally.

"I'm on my way there now. Why? What's the deal?" Golden asked. "Cool. Fifty bands for you, and twenty for homeboy with the blood. I got that faded all day. I thought you were finna tell me some bad shit."

Golden swapped a few more words with Dr. Abagnale and then he hollered at the twins for a minute. After he hung up with them, he focused his attention on the streets, speeding toward his destination.

***

Wood, Hush, and Boodee were eating inside of a hood Chinese food spot when Remo entered, causing the bell hanging over the door to ring. Wood kept his eyes on him as he walked up to the window and ordered his food. He paid for his order, took his ticket stub, and walked over to the table. He shook up with Hush and Boodee, but Wood left him hanging. Remo didn't take the shit to heart, he sat at the table, declining the house special Chow Mein Boodee offered him.

"I'm good, B, I just ordered some shit," Remo said.

He looked at Wood, who was washing down his food with a Coca-Cola. He wiped his mouth with a napkin and started back eating.

"What did you call us here for that's so important?" Wood asked.

"Ya boy, Rich Loc, I've got an address," Remo placed a card on the table and slid it before Wood.

Wood sat his box of Chinese food down and looked over the card. His eyes lit up with mischief as he smiled wickedly and thumped the card.

***

Golden drove up across the street from Dr. Abagnale's crib in time to see an old automobile driving away from the curb. He wasn't sure of its make and model, but it looked like one of those throwback cars from the Harlem Nights movie. He grabbed his backpack from the front passenger seat and jogged across the street. He walked around to the back of Dr. Abagnale's house and shot him a text message to open the backdoor.

Baby Girl opened the backdoor and gave him a brotherly hug. His heart dropped like he was riding a roller coaster when he saw her glassy-red eyes and wet cheeks. He feared his mother had died while he was gone. The thought of losing his old girl made him want to throw up. He started to feel queasy.

"Baby Girl, what's the deal? Momma okay?" Golden asked, placing his hand on her shoulder.

Golden didn't know why it seemed like it took forever for Baby Girl to answer, but it was driving him insane. "Dr.

Abagnale said that ma's gonna be okay, but those bullets she took did a real number on her. She's gonna need surgery to save her arm and leg. And even if the operation is successful, she won't walk the same way or be able to move her arm like she used to." Baby Girl broke down sobbing and buried her face into Golden's shirt.

He comforted her the best way he could, assuring her that everything was going to be alright. "Come on now, sis, you know maduke's a beast. She gon' get through this shit, and be back in the trenches, like she didn't just take two from a choppa. Watch. You'll see."

Using the lower half of his shirt, Golden dried Baby Girl's face and kissed her forehead. "Yo, you know who was whippin' that old joint outside that looked like it was from the 1930's, or some shit?" he inquired.

"Probably that blood dealer," Baby Girl said, sniffling. "He was dressed real snazzy, like people were in that era, maybe even earlier. I don't know what it was about 'em, he looked really young, but hadda old school vibe to 'em. You know what I mean?"

"Yeah. I think so."

Golden hung his arm around Baby Girl's shoulder and they walked down inside the basement. Shirvetta was lying in the same he'd left her, only she was talking to someone on her cellphone. Meanwhile, Dr. Abagnale was busy applying the dressing to Biggie's wounded eye. Golden knocked on the wall to announce his presence. He walked past Dr. Abagnale and dumped the money for his services and the blood packs on a table on the opposite side of the basement.

"Baby, Golden just came down with Baby Girl. You still wanna holla at 'em?" Shirvetta said into her cellphone. She held the cellular to her chest and motioned Golden over. "Golden, your father wants to talk to you."

Golden took the cellphone from his mother and walked to a corner of the basement. "What up, pop?"

"Yo' momma told me what went down today," Heavy began. "Son, I'm not out there in the free world to give them busta ass niggaz what they deserve for touchin' mine, so the responsibility falls on yo' shoulders. You send them marks a message, you let 'em know that when they fuck with the queen, they feel the wrath of the whole hive. You hear me, son?"

"I got it, pop. And on my soul, niggaz gon' answer for what they did to our queen," Golden said, looking over his shoulder at his mother. She had Baby Girl and Dr. Abagnale moving around her preparing her for the blood transfusion. "Yeah. I'll be sure to keep you updated. I love you, too, O.G. Peace." Golden disconnected the call and gave the cell back to his mother. He grasped her hand affectionately and kissed her gently on the forehead. "I love you, old lady."

"I love you, too, son," Shirvetta smiled.

Golden plopped down on the brown leather couch and took a breath. It had been a long day, and he was exhausted. Biggie sat down beside him. He could tell he was just as exhausted as he was. He hugged him into his side and kissed the top of his head.

"I love you, Big," Golden told him.

"I love you, too, big bruh," Biggie replied, yawning.

"Family is all we've got, my G. You gotta put this shit between you and Cow behind y'all." Biggie didn't answer, so he addressed him again. "Biggie, you hear me?" Biggie snored loudly. The young nigga had fallen asleep just that quick.

Baby Girl hugged Golden around his neck and kissed him on the cheek. They exchanged "I love you's", she threw on her hood, and laid her head in his lap. Yawning, she closed her eyes and drifted off to sleep.

A slight smirk accented the corner of Golden's lips as he looked at the twins. He thought about Cowboy, his mother, his father, and the love of his life, Aries. He loved them with all his heart and every last inch of his soul. He was willing to go to war with anyone on the map behind them.

Golden looked at his mother as Dr. Abagnale was fixing her arm with a needle for the blood transfusion. Shirvetta smiled at her second-oldest son and blew him a kiss. He hit her with the smile he used to give her when he was a little boy, and she'd let him lick the frosting off a wire whip. Shirvetta's smile grew faint as she fell asleep. Golden yawned and smacked his lips. His vision became blurry and his eyelids felt like dumbbells. He fought to stay awake, but eventually, the Sandman won.

***

Dr. Abagnale was asking for two hundred thousand dollars to perform the surgery Shirvetta would need to save her arm and leg. Golden had about a hundred twenty thousand left in his bag, so he left him with that and a promise to give him the other eighty thousand the day of the surgery. With the recent shootout with Rich Loc and his locs, Golden knew they'd be scouring the streets for his family, so he figured it was best for his mother to stay at one of the armories. He and the twins took her to one twenty minutes away from the one where he was staying. The difference between this armory and the one Golden was staying in, this one had a security system and surveillance cameras that allowed the residents to see everything on the outside.

Golden planned on setting his mother up in the basement, since it was bulletproof, bombproof, and made up like one of those luxury Hollywood apartments. The basement door was made of iron and no one could access it unless they had the code and a verified thumbprint. After getting Shirvetta settled in the bedroom, Golden and the twins kissed her goodnight and left her to get some rest.

Biggie pulled out his gun and sat it on the bartop as he sat down on a stool. "Aye, sis, why don't chu fix yo' twin a drink."

"Why not? I could use one my-damn-self." Baby Girl walked around to the opposite side of the bar. "You want a drink, Golden?" she asked, grabbing the liquor bottles to make her and Biggie's favorite drink.

"Nah, I'm good, sis," Golden said with a frown, texting Aries back. He'd been swapping texts with her since they'd left Dr. Abagnale's crib. She'd told him the deal with Rich Loc, and he told her what popped off between them earlier that day. Now he was hitting her back, telling her to whack his ass right then for him, in code of course.

Golden plopped down on the couch and waited for Aries' to hit him back. He was hoping she'd go through with taking Rich Loc out, so he wouldn't have to. She could make shit easy for him, if she did this one little favor for him. She claimed that she would, but something within his heart told him she wouldn't do it because she had feelings for the nigga.

Come on, shorty, do yo' shit. Prove to me you love me more than you do this nigga, Golden thought. *If she doesn't drill 'em then I may have to do her. It's like Cow said, homie could put a battery in her back and send her to peel my onion.*

Golden leaned his head back and took a deep breath. He stared up at the ceiling, thinking and halfway listening to the twins converse.

"Golden."

Golden was so wrapped up in his thoughts he didn't reply.

"Golden. Golden!"

Golden snapped out of it and looked at Baby Girl. "Yeah?"

146

"Where were you just now?" Baby Girl asked and took a sip of her drink.

"Shit. I don't know," Golden sat up on the couch. "What's the deal tho?"

"You think ma is gonna be okay?" Baby Girl asked.

"No doubt. Abagnale is droppin' by tomorrow for her surgery," Golden informed her. "Once that's a wrap, she'll just need time to relax and build her strength back up. She'll be good."

Biggie picked up his drink and walked over to Golden. "See there? I told you not to worry, sis. Ma is gonna be a'ight."

Baby Girl sat down beside Golden and laid her head against his shoulder. "I really hope so, twin. I really do."

Golden was about to say something when his cellular chimed with a text. He glanced at the message and became angry and hurt, at the same time. Biggie, who was sitting beside him, saw the expression on his face and looked over at the screen of his cellphone. He understood wholeheartedly why his brother was looking how he was now.

Aries: *Again, I'm sorry, I couldn't find any red balloons. I hope you find it in your heart to forgive me.*

"Aries couldn't bring herself to whack who? Rich Loc?" Biggie inquired.

Golden nodded.

"She musta caught feelings." Baby Girl shook her head and took a sip of her drink.

Golden blew his frustration. "Yep."

Biggie took a sip of his drink and licked his lips. "That's all bad, big bruh. I love sis, but I love my blood more," he assured him. "I think it's best that chu allow me to, uh, you know."

Off of Biggie's facial expression, Golden knew, just like Cowboy, he was willing to take Aries out, on his behalf. A part of him wanted to give him the go ahead to lay down his murder game, but the other part of him was hoping to salvage his relationship.

Golden shook his head. "Nah, baby bruh, I got this one. You and sis just worry about taking care of ma." He got up from the couch, putting away his cellphone. "As y'all know, Abagnale is gonna be expecting eighty bands tomorrow for ma's operation. So, one of y'all will have to get the combo for her safe and get the bread, preferably before he gets here."

Biggie nodded and said, "I can fade that."

"Cool. I'll stay back and hold down, ma."

"Big, I want chu to holla at Cow and squash y'all shit," Golden told Biggie.

Biggie was silent for what seemed like forever to Golden, before he said something. "Look, Gold, I'm not makin' any promises, but I'll think about it."

"Hey, comin' from you, lil bruh, that's progress," Golden replied, turning to walk away. "I love y'all."

"We love you, too," Baby Girl said, as he walked up the staircase. "Where you going now?"

"To check up on Cow," Golden yelled back, as he disappeared up the staircase.

Chapter 23

The air was thick with anticipation as Golden made his way to the front door, the aroma of Cowboy's favorite fast food teasing his senses. He couldn't wait to surprise his brother, knowing how much this simple gesture would mean to him.

"Yo, Cow, I'm back, baby, and guess what I got," Golden said, looking around as he walked through the living room. Excitement bubbled inside his chest, as he drew closer to Cowboy's bedroom. He was about to knock on his door, but what he heard next made him pause with concern.

Frowning, Golden pressed his ear against the door, straining to hear any sound from inside. That's when he heard it—the soft murmur of Cowboy's voice, speaking as if to someone only he could see. Golden's heart clenched at the realization that Cowboy was talking to his deceased mother again.

***

"They just left me out there, momma. How can they leave me to die, and I'm 'posed to be family?" Cowboy complained with teary eyes.

"Awww, come here, baby," Chick sat on the bed beside her son and laid the side of his face against her chest. She kissed the top of his head and rubbed his back comfortingly, rocking back and forth.

"I swear to God, momma. No one has ever really loved me besides you," Cowboy told her, wiping the wetness from his eyes.

"That's right, son, and momma is all you'll ever need," Chick replied. "I gotcho back and you've got my front. It's us against the world, fuck everyone else."

Cowboy looked up at her with his sad, childlike eyes, and called for her attention, "Momma."

"Yes, sweetness."

"Can you, can you sing that song you used to sing to me when I was lil, please?"

"Sure, baby boy. Close your eyes."

Cowboy closed his eyes and his mother sang to him, just like she did when he was a little boy. A smirk graced his lips and shortly he fell asleep. Chick laid him down on his stomach, caressed the side of his head, and kissed him on his temple. She walked over to the bedroom door and turned back around to him.

"Sweet dreams, prince, soon I'll step in and make everyone that ever hurt chu pay," Chick told him as he snored softly. She turned off the light and pulled the door shut as she walked out of the bedroom. "I swear it, on my grave."

Golden walked briskly down the hallway and dumped the Jersey Mike's bag on the kitchen table. He moved swiftly, sneakers squeaking against the linoleum. He gathered everything he deemed potentially dangerous. Knives, forks, meat tenderizer, and guns were stashed away, medications were secured, and sharp objects were hidden from sight.

Golden had just put away the last item that posed a threat to Cowboy's life, when he heard his footsteps approaching. He turned around in time to see Cowboy emerge through the kitchen door. He wore an expression of exhaustion on his face, but his heart tinged with remorse.

"Say, G," he said softly, his voice heavy with guilt. "I'm sorry about the other day."

Golden met his brother's gaze, his eyes softening with understanding. "It's okay, bro," he replied gently, presenting him with a reassuring smile. "Let's just enjoy tonight, a'ight? I gotcho fave sub." He held up the Jersey Mike's bag. "Supreme club sub on cheese and rosemary bread, made Mike's way, with avocado and crisp bacon. Just like you like it, my boy."

Cowboy stifled through the sandwich bag until he found his sub, a 20oz A&W Root Beer, and a bag of Ruffles potato chips. He was smiling like he found the prize inside a cereal box.

"Yo, son, I'm bouta beat this shit down," Cowboy said excitedly, he couldn't wait to have his way with the sandwich.

Golden grabbed his sub and his Canada Dry out of the Jersey Mike's bag. He threw his head toward the living room. "Come on, bruh, all of the seasons of Martin are on Netflix. I figure, we can stuff our faces and laugh our asses off."

"Rent 'em Spoons," Cowboy shouted, mocking Cole from the Martin television show.

He and Golden sat down before their sandwiches and unwrapped them. As the brothers ate, the tension from the other day melted and was replaced by the comfort of familiar food and each other's company. Eventually, exhaustion caught up with Cowboy, and his eyelids became heavy with sleep. Golden watched over him, acting like a silent guardian in the glow of the television's screen. He draped a blanket over Cowboy's slumbering form and kissed his forehead.

"Goodnight, big bro," he whispered, voice dripping affection and warmth.

After turning off the television, Golden walked down the hallway to the other bedroom to get himself some sleep.

***

The sun shined on Cowboy's face, and he squinted. His eyes fluttered open. He moved to dig the boogers out the corners of his eyes and something snagged his wrist. Frowning, he looked at his wrist and it was in a metal shackle, chained to the wall.

"What the fuck?" he said under his breath, scrambling to get off the couch. His legs got tangled in the blanket and he fell on the floor. Pulling himself back up on his feet, he yanked and yanked at the chain, but it held fast. He looked around the living room, but he didn't see Golden anywhere. Now he was worried. "Golden? Golden. Golllllldennnn!"

Cowboy didn't receive a response, so he went back to yanking at the chain, hoping it would come out of the wall, but unfortunately, it wouldn't budge. He kept at it, until he was shiny with sweat and breathing hard. Sitting on the floor against the couch, he took in his surroundings and saw a folded sheet of paper with his name on it. His forehead wrinkled wondering what could have been written on it. He snatched the paper off the coffee table and read over it in whispers.

What up, Cow?

By the time you read this, I'll be on my way back home. I know when you woke up you were like, what the fuck? When you saw I'd chained you to the living room wall. I also hid everything inside the house I thought you could use to hurt yourself, or someone else. I know you're probably cussing me out right now, but I did what I did because I love and care about you. Don't trip though. I'm not leaving you there to die. I'll be back soon. And when I do, we're going to see about getting you some help. That mental health shit is not a joke and should be taken very seriously. I promise you; I'm going to do everything in my power to make sure you're good. I love you, big bruh, and nothing and no one will ever change that.

Your little bro, Golden

P.S. I sat a lunch box with food and water on the coffee table. I also left buckets for you to shit and piss in.

Peace.

"Son of a bitch!" Cowboy balled up the sheet of paper and threw across the living room. He kicked the coffee table and knocked the lunch pail to the floor. He threw a tantrum like a fucking four year old, swinging in the air and kicking over the buckets. He went on and on until he was exhausted, with sweat bubbles on his forehead. He lay awkwardly on the floor, staring up at the ceiling, with his heart racing.

***

Golden removed his motorcycle helmet as he approached the front door of the armory and let himself inside. He verified his identity at the scanner, punched in the access code, and the basement door clicked open. He reached the landing and found his family lounging on the couches. He'd called an emergency meeting when he'd gotten halfway home from Connecticut. His conversation with Cowboy was still fresh on his mind, and he wanted to get everything out there.

Golden hit up his father, put the jack on speaker once he answered, and placed his cellphone on the coffee table, beside his motorcycle helmet.

"Pop's you still there?" Golden asked.

"Yeah, I'm still here. What's on yo' mind, son?"

"I hollered at big bruh the other day, and he had a lot to say," Golden informed him. "I wanna ask you and ma some questions, and with all due respect, I don't wanna hear no bullshit," he said, with a dead serious look in his eyes.

The twins exchanged glances when they saw the look on their brother's face. They knew right then he didn't come there to play games, he wanted the truth.

Golden stole a look at Shirvetta and she had a face of stone. The expression she had made him second guess the validity of Cowboy's story. He checked himself on the spot. He forgot he was dealing with a seasoned veteran. The O.G. knew how to hide her feelings, when it came to questioning, and she'd taught her offspring the same.

The entire basement was in silence, until Heavy spoke up.

"Go ahead and put it on the table, son. We're all here."

Heavy, Shirvetta, and the twins were all ears as Golden told them how the disappearance of Cowboy's mother had affected him. The tale left Biggie fighting with the feelings he had toward Cowboy, while Baby Girl dropped a few tears. Shirvetta, on the other hand, was stoic and didn't show any sign of sympathy for her stepson. Golden knew then that she was guilty of dropping Cowboy's mother, but he had to hear it from her lips. He had to hear her say that she had rocked his big brother's ma-dukes asleep.

Golden watched his mother, like he was examining her from behind the lens of a microscope, as he relayed what happened between her and Chick the night she was murdered. He then popped the million-dollar question that had been plaguing his mind.

"Son, I can tell you now, that's not the way things happened," Heavy spoke up.

"Pardon me, pop, but I wanna hear what ma has to say about all of this," Golden replied, eyes still glued on his mother.

"Well, ma?" Baby Girl said, looking at her mother.

"Yo, G, you really wildin' to even ask ma somethin' like that," Biggie threw in his two cents. "You gettin' at moms about some bullshit story our junkie ass brother cooked up.

We all know what happened to Cowboy's O.G., her deadbeat ass skipped town, most likely with some paypa'd up dope boy, fa all we know."

"Biggie, do me a favor." Biggie looked at Golden like, *what's up*? "Shut the fuck up, and let ma answer the question. How about it, ma, did you drop big bro's old lady behind Pop, like he said you did?"

Chapter 24

The basement was so quiet all they could hear was the ticking of the clock on the wall and the buzzing of a fly, swarming around aimlessly. Golden didn't bat an eye, as he waited for his mother's response, alongside the twins. His heart started racing like he'd eaten an edible, and he found himself having a little trouble breathing.

"Alright, you wanna know if I killed yo' brother's mother or not? The answer is yes," Shirvetta admitted, stunning everyone around her. "Yes. I killed that bitch. And had I not done what I did, we wouldn't have the family we have now."

"Ma, noooo." Baby Girl looked at her mother in disbelief.

Biggie couldn't say shit. The revelation was like a punch to his gut, and he felt like the wind had been knocked out of him.

Golden stared at Shirvetta seething, nostrils flared, lips twisted, tears dripping from his eyes.

"Oh, don't look at me like that, Golden," Shirvetta scrunched her face. She couldn't believe her children had the reaction they had when she'd done what she did for them. "Chick had yo' daddy under her spell. I knew he'd never let her go, unless she was outta the picture. You know what? I'll be damn if I sit here and let y'all make me feel bad, when I did right by y'all. Y'all should be lined up to kiss my ass right now 'cause it's 'cause of me you had a full time daddy in ya life."

156

"I can't believe you, ma. I need a drink!" Baby Girl shot to her feet, storming over to the bar to make herself a drink. She tapped her foot heatedly as she tossed back the alcohol and poured herself another shot.

"Boy, I wasn't ready for this shit tonight. I need a cigarette, and bad, too," Shirvetta said to no one in particular, taking a pack of Newports from inside of her homemade sling. She placed a cigarette between her lips and requested a light from Biggie. After he obliged her request, she took a hit and blew out a cloud of smoke. She swept her hair out of her face and looked at Golden. He looked like a raging beast that couldn't wait to be let out of its cage.

"Pop, are you there? Pop?" Biggie picked up Golden's cellphone. "He hung up," he announced, looking from his brother to his mother. He could tell Golden was dealing with a bout of emotional turmoil.

Shirvetta took the cigarette out of her mouth and blew a cloud of smoke. "Why are you lookin' at me like that?"

Golden opened his mouth to say something, but his feelings choked him. He took the time to gather himself before trying to speak again. "You fucked up Cowboy's life. He's all screwed up now, and it's all 'cause of you." Tears collected in his eyes and rolled down his face. "My big brother is broken so bad, I don't know if I can even fix 'em, but I'm gonna try. I'm never gonna give up on 'em."

Golden grabbed his helmet and pocketed his cellphone. He started up the staircase, but turned around when his mother called after him.

Shirvetta pulled herself up from the couch with her walking cane. "You only get one mother, son. I want chu to remember that."

Golden glared at her for a moment and continued up the staircase.

"Sis, pour me a shot, would ya?" Biggie asked Baby Girl. He walked toward the bar beside his mother, in case she needed his assistance. As soon as they sat at the bar, Baby Girl gave them both a shot each.

Shirvetta watched her youngest children throw back the shots of alcohol. Baby Girl refilled the glasses and they carried on, like she wasn't even there. Shirvetta was expecting them to come at her with a barrage of questions, and it was driving her up the wall that they hadn't.

"Okay. Come on with it." Shirvetta blew out smoke and mashed her cigarette out on the bar top. The twins looked at her with clueless expressions on their faces. "About me closin' the curtains on Cowboy's biological mother's show."

"There really ain't much more to say, ma. You know what chu did is messed up, and so do Biggie and I," Baby Girl said. She was still trying to figure out how to handle the news. If it hadn't come from her own mother's lips that she bodied her oldest brother's mother, then she would have never believed it.

Shirvetta turned to Biggie. "And you?"

Biggie took a breath and slumped his shoulders. "Like Baby Girl said, what chu did to bruh moms is messed up. I know if I was in bro's shoes, I'd be plottin' how to do you in.   Real   talk."
"Oh, best believe that's exactly what that crazy mothafucka's doin', plottin'," Shirvetta assured him. "You heard what Golden said he told 'em. That was clearly a threat. Can we all agree on that?" She looked at the twins, and they nodded in agreement. "Good. Look, I'm on the injured list right now, so it's gonna be up to y'all two to get this thing done."

Baby Girl's forehead wrinkled. "Get what thing done?"

"I think we all know what I'm talkin' about here. But if you need me to come out and say it, I will," Shirvetta said. "You two are gonna take out Cowboy."

"Ma, are you serious?" Baby Girl asked.

"Oh, yes, I am, so I need you to take this situation just like that, seriously," Shirvetta replied. She then turned to Biggie, rubbing the back of his head. "How about it, baby boy? Can I count on you?"

Biggie reluctantly nodded. After popping all that shit about killing Cowboy, now that he got the greenlight, he had cold feet. He knew his mother's life was in danger, as long as Cowboy was alive, and if push came to shove, he would use his love for her to carry out his execution.

"I hate to put it to you like this, sweetie, but you're gonna have to make a choice," Shirvetta started back up with Baby Girl. "Now, it's either gonna be me, or ya brother. If I were you, I'd choose me, 'cause even with Junior gone, you'll still have two brothers left."

Baby Girl looked at her mother in shock. She couldn't believe what she'd just said to her. It was fucked the fuck up, but she was absolutely right. She had to make a choice.

"So, what's it gonna be?" Shirvetta asked. She looked upon her with pleading eyes, hoping she'd be down with the assassination.

Baby Girl bowed her head and big teardrops fell from her eyes. She wiped them away and looked back up at Shirvetta, nodding.

"That's my girl. I knew you wouldn't let cho mother down." Shirvetta grinned, reaching across the bar and hugging her with her good arm. She kissed her forehead, turned to Biggie, and gave him the same form of affection.

***

Heavy splashed water on his face and stared at his reflection in the metal reflector. The past had finally come back to bite him in his ass. He didn't have any idea how he was going to handle his situation, so he figured it was best he slept on it. He laid down on his mattress with his fingers

159

interlocked behind his head. He knew, without a doubt, there was going to be one hell of a war on the streets, and unfortunately, it was going to be waged between his children. What was even more fucked up was he wasn't free to stop the war from happening. His only hope was that Golden could stop his blood from spilling its own blood. It was a long shot, but it was the only way he could see the issue being resolved.

I know it's a lot for you to deal with, youngin', but I pray to God that you can pull it off.

***

Chris Stacks' nurse threw a big towel and a washcloth over her shoulder and picked up the bassinet of sudsy hot water. She walked down the corridor, singing softly.

"Where you going, Mercy?" one of the nurses asked, as she passed her.

"To give my patient a bath," Nurse Mercy replied.

"Oh. Well, have fun," the nurse said, turning left at the end of the hallway.

Nurse Mercy walked into Chris Stacks' room and flipped on the light switch. She pulled the curtain back and his bed was empty. But it still held the mold of his body. Nurse Mercy dropped the bassinet and sudsy water spilled everywhere. She looked under the bed and checked the bathroom, but he wasn't there either. She slipped on the water she spilt running toward the door, but scrambled back up on her sneakers. Running out into the corridor, she hollered for the attention of the rest of the hospital staff on her wing.

The elevator stopped on the garage floor, and its double doors opened. Hush, who was wearing a mask over his mouth and blue scrubs, emerged, pushing a wheelchair with

Chris Stacks slumped in it. He had on a big straw hat and a blanket was draped over him. He slowly came out of his coma as he was rolled through the parking lot. Frowning, he lifted his head and stared at the blurry image in front of him. As his vision came back to normal, so did what was before his eyes. It was Boodee standing at the rear of the Suburban, smoking a cigarette. When he saw Chris Stacks, he dropped the burning cancer stick at his foot and mashed it out. He then opened the backdoor of the truck and stood aside so Chris could get in.

Chris Stacks didn't know who the fuck Boodee was, so he knew his situation couldn't be good. He thrashed around in the wheelchair, trying desperately to get out, but to no avail. His wheelchair suddenly stopped, and Hush stepped in front of him, pulling his mask down.

"You can try as hard as you want, but yo' ass ain't gettin' outta this one," Hush told him and snatched off the blanket, like he was revealing something. Chris Stacks had duct tape over his mouth and his wrists and ankles were duct taped to the wheelchair. He threw his head back, trying to scream for help, and his hat fell off.

Hush punched him in the chin and knocked him out cold. He then motioned Boodee over. "Help me get this muthafucka in the backseat, B."

Boodee cut the duct tape from Chris Stacks' wrists and ankles and then pocketed his Swiss army knife. Hush grabbed him underneath his arms, while Boodee grabbed hold of his legs. After they deposited him into the backseat, they hopped inside the Suburban and drove out of the garage.

***

The last time Golden was laid up with Aries, he placed a tracking application on her cellular, so he'd know where she was at all times. He was hoping Aries would have bodied

Rich Loc, so he wouldn't have to use the app, but unfortunately, things didn't work out that way.

Golden parked his car in the backyard of his parent's house and pulled out his Kawasaki Ninja 400 motorcycle. He slipped his helmet over his head, adjusted it, and turned the key in the ignition. The bike came to life, and he revved it up. It squealed annoyingly loud. He took off down the driveway, made a right at the end of it, and zipped up the block.

Golden made it back to the armory, where he'd stashed his money from the Rich Loc lick, and got dressed in a red leather motorcycle jumpsuit. He went into the small study, pulled a thick green book downward, and the bookshelf slid back inside the wall. A neon blue light popped on, revealing a room loaded with a cache of weapons hanging on every wall. Entering the room, Golden took his time looking over the variety of guns, like they were the blueprint to some sort of machine he planned to build. He found the weapon he was looking for and took it down, checking the sights on it. It was a modified P-90 Herstal submachine gun. He also strapped a bowie knife to his thigh and strapped a holstered .380 semi-automatic pistol to his ankle.

Golden took one more look at his cellphone for Aries's location, as he stepped out of the house. He slipped his cell back inside his pocket, shut the visor of his helmet, and mounted his Kawasaki Ninja. He flew down the block, leaving debris in his wake.

***

"A'ight, shorty, I'm finna get outta here. Gemme a kiss," Rich Loc tucked his gun at the small of his back and pulled her close. Aries cupped his face and kissed him twice.

"I love you," Aries told him.

"I love you, too. Don't forget to drop that package off to Rollins," Rich Loc replied, picking up the duffle bags. Parelli was driving him around to the families of the locs who lost their lives, so he could give them enough dough for themselves and to pay for their loved ones' funerals.

"I won't."

Aries shut the front door behind him and locked it. She walked back toward the master bedroom to get dressed and spotted Rich Loc's keys on the dining room table. Snatching his keys, she ran out onto the front porch, but Rich Loc was already gone. Walking back inside the house, she sent him a text to let him know he'd forgotten his keys. Afterward, she got dressed, wrapped up half of a kilo, and placed it inside her oversized designer purse. Hearing someone honking outside, she figured it was Rich Loc coming back to retrieve his keys.

"That man would forget his head if it wasn't attached to his neck." Aries smiled, grabbing the designer bag and Rich Loc's keys. She walked back to the front of the house and looked through the curtains to make sure it was Rich Loc outside.

***

Golden sped through the New York City streets, like he had the road all to himself. He cut it close, tailgating, and dipping in and out of lanes. Coming off the highway, he slowed to the speed limit and made his way to his destination. He stopped his motorcycle outside of Rich Loc's crib, drew his P-90 Herstal submachine gun, and blew his horn. He pointed his weapon at the window he believed Rich Loc would look out from and waited for him to appear. As soon as the curtain was pulled back from the window, Golden squeezed the trigger and a burst of flames spat out of his weapon's barrel.

To Be Concluded...

Lock Down Publications and Ca$h Presents
Assisted Publishing Packages

BASIC PACKAGE	UPGRADED PACKAGE
$499	$800
Editing	Typing
Cover Design	Editing
Formatting	Cover Design
	Formatting
ADVANCE PACKAGE	**LDP SUPREME PACKAGE**
$1,200	$1,500
Typing	Typing
Editing	Editing
Cover Design	Cover Design
Formatting	Formatting
Copyright registration	Copyright registration
Proofreading	Proofreading
Upload book to Amazon	Set up Amazon account
	Upload book to Amazon
	Advertise on LDP, Amazon and Facebook Page

***Other services available upon request.
Additional charges may apply

Lock Down Publications
P.O. Box 944
Stockbridge, GA 30281-9998
Phone: 470 303-9761

Submission Guideline

Submit the first three chapters of your completed manuscript to ldpsubmissions@gmail.com. In the subject line add **Your Book's Title**. The manuscript must be in a Word Doc file and sent as an attachment. Document should be in Times New Roman, double spaced, and in size 12 font. Also, provide your synopsis and full contact information. If sending multiple submissions, they must each be in a separate email.

Have a story but no way to send it electronically? You can still submit to LDP/Ca$h Presents. Send in the first three chapters, written or typed, of your completed manuscript to:

LDP: Submissions Dept
P.O. Box 944
Stockbridge, GA 30281-9998

DO NOT send original manuscript. Must be a duplicate. Provide your synopsis and a cover letter containing your full contact information.

Thanks for considering LDP and Ca$h Presents.

NEW RELEASES

BLOODLINE OF A SAVAGE 1&2
THESE VICIOUS STREETS 1&2
RELENTLESS GOON
RELENTLESS GOON 2
BY PRINCE A. TAUHID

THE BUTTERFLY MAFIA 1-3
BY FUMIYA PAYNE

A THUG'S STREET PRINCESS 1&2
BY MEESHA

CITY OF SMOKE 2
BY MOLOTTI

STEPPERS 1,2&3
THE REAL BADDIES OF CHI-RAQ
BY KING RIO

THE LANE 1&2
BY KEN-KEN SPENCE

THUG OF SPADES 1&2
LOVE IN THE TRENCHES 2
CORNER BOYS
BY COREY ROBINSON

TIL DEATH 3
BY ARYANNA

THE BIRTH OF A GANGSTER 4
BY DELMONT PLAYER

PRODUCT OF THE STREETS 1&2
BY DEMOND "MONEY" ANDERSON

NO TIME FOR ERROR
BY KEESE

MONEY HUNGRY DEMONS
BY TRANAY ADAMS

Coming Soon from Lock Down Publications/Ca$h Presents

IF YOU CROSS ME ONCE 6
ANGEL V
By Anthony Fields

IMMA DIE BOUT MINE 5
By Aryanna

A THUGS STREET PRINCESS 3
By Meesha

PRODUCT OF THE STREETS 3
By Demond Money Anderson

CORNER BOYS 2
By Corey Robinson

THE MURDER QUEENS 6&7
By Michael Gallon

CITY OF SMOKE 3
By Molotti

CONFESSIONS OF A DOPE BOY
By Nicholas Lock

THA TAKEOVER
By Keith Chandler

BETRAYAL OF A G 2
By Ray Vinci

CRIME BOSS
By Playa Ray

Available Now

RESTRAINING ORDER 1 & 2
By **CA$H & Coffee**

LOVE KNOWS NO BOUNDARIES 1-3
By **Coffee**

RAISED AS A GOON I, II, III & IV
BRED BY THE SLUMS I, II, III
BLAST FOR ME I & II
ROTTEN TO THE CORE I II III
A BRONX TALE I, II, III
DUFFLE BAG CARTEL I II III IV V VI
HEARTLESS GOON I II III IV V
A SAVAGE DOPEBOY I II
DRUG LORDS I II III
CUTTHROAT MAFIA I II
KING OF THE TRENCHES
By **Ghost**

LAY IT DOWN I & II
LAST OF A DYING BREED I II
BLOOD STAINS OF A SHOTTA I & II III
By **Jamaica**

LOYAL TO THE GAME I II III
LIFE OF SIN I, II III
By **TJ & Jelissa**

IF LOVING HIM IS WRONG...I & II
LOVE ME EVEN WHEN IT HURTS I II III
By **Jelissa**

PUSH IT TO THE LIMIT
By **Bre' Hayes**

BLOODY COMMAS I & II
SKI MASK CARTEL I, II & III
KING OF NEW YORK I II, III IV V
RISE TO POWER I II III
COKE KINGS I II III IV V
BORN HEARTLESS I II III IV
KING OF THE TRAP I II
By **T.J. Edwards**

WHEN THE STREETS CLAP BACK I & II III
THE HEART OF A SAVAGE I II III IV
MONEY MAFIA I II
LOYAL TO THE SOIL I II III
By **Jibril Williams**

A DISTINGUISHED THUG STOLE MY HEART I II & III
LOVE SHOULDN'T HURT I II III IV
RENEGADE BOYS 1-4
PAID IN KARMA 1-3
SAVAGE STORMS 1-3
AN UNFORESEEN LOVE 1-3
BABY, I'M WINTERTIME COLD 1-3
A THUG'S STREET PRINCESS 1&2
By **Meesha**

A GANGSTER'S CODE 1-3
A GANGSTER'S SYN 1-3
THE SAVAGE LIFE 1-3
CHAINED TO THE STREETS 1-3
BLOOD ON THE MONEY 1-3
A GANGSTA'S PAIN 1-3
BEAUTIFUL LIES AND UGLY TRUTHS
CHURCH IN THESE STREETS
By **J-Blunt**

CUM FOR ME 1-8
An LDP Erotica Collaboration

BLOOD OF A BOSS 1-5
SHADOWS OF THE GAME
TRAP BASTARD
By **Askari**

THE STREETS BLEED MURDER 1-3
THE HEART OF A GANGSTA 1-3
By **Jerry Jackson**

WHEN A GOOD GIRL GOES BAD
By **Adrienne**

THE COST OF LOYALTY 1-3
By **Kweli**

BRIDE OF A HUSTLA 1-3
THE FETTI GIRLS 1-3
CORRUPTED BY A GANGSTA 1-4
BLINDED BY HIS LOVE
THE PRICE YOU PAY FOR LOVE 1-3
DOPE GIRL MAGIC 1-3
By **Destiny Skai**

A KINGPIN'S AMBITION
A KINGPIN'S AMBITION II
I MURDER FOR THE DOUGH
By **Ambitious**

TRUE SAVAGE 1-7
DOPE BOY MAGIC 1-3
MIDNIGHT CARTEL 1-3
CITY OF KINGZ 1&2
NIGHTMARE ON SILENT AVE
THE PLUG OF LIL MEXICO 1&2
CLASSIC CITY
By **Chris Green**

A GANGSTER'S REVENGE 1-4
THE BOSS MAN'S DAUGHTERS 1-5
A SAVAGE LOVE 1&2
BAE BELONGS TO ME 1&2
A HUSTLER'S DECEIT 1-3
WHAT BAD BITCHES DO 1-3
SOUL OF A MONSTER 1-3
KILL ZONE
A DOPE BOY'S QUEEN 1-3
TIL DEATH 1-3
IMMA DIE BOUT MINE 1-4
By **Aryanna**

A DOPEBOY'S PRAYER
By **Eddie "Wolf" Lee**

THE KING CARTEL 1-3
By **Frank Gresham**

THESE NIGGAS AIN'T LOYAL 1-3
By **Nikki Tee**

GANGSTA SHYT 1-3
By **CATO**

THE ULTIMATE BETRAYAL
By **Phoenix**

BOSS'N UP 1-3
By **Royal Nicole**

I LOVE YOU TO DEATH
By **Destiny J**

I RIDE FOR MY HITTA
I STILL RIDE FOR MY HITTA
By **Misty Holt**

LOVE & CHASIN' PAPER
By **Qay Crockett**

TO DIE IN VAIN
SINS OF A HUSTLA
By **ASAD**

BROOKLYN HUSTLAZ
By **Boogsy Morina**

BROOKLYN ON LOCK 1 & 2
By **Sonovia**

GANGSTA CITY
By **Teddy Duke**

A DRUG KING AND HIS DIAMOND 1-3
A DOPEMAN'S RICHES
HER MAN, MINE'S TOO 1&2
CASH MONEY HO'S
THE WIFEY I USED TO BE 1&2
PRETTY GIRLS DO NASTY THINGS
By **Nicole Goosby**

LIPSTICK KILLAH 1-3
CRIME OF PASSION 1-3
FRIEND OR FOE 1-3
By **Mimi**

TRAPHOUSE KING 1-3
KINGPIN KILLAZ 1-3
STREET KINGS 1&2
PAID IN BLOOD 1&2
CARTEL KILLAZ 1-3
DOPE GODS 1&2
By **Hood Rich**

THE STREETS ARE CALLING
By **Duquie Wilson**

STEADY MOBBN' 1-3
THE STREETS STAINED MY SOUL 1-3
By **Marcellus Allen**

WHO SHOT YA 1-3
SON OF A DOPE FIEND 1-4
HEAVEN GOT A GHETTO 1&2
SKI MASK MONEY 1&2
By **Renta**

GORILLAZ IN THE BAY 1-4
TEARS OF A GANGSTA 1/&2
3X KRAZY 1&2
STRAIGHT BEAST MODE 1&2
By **DE'KARI**

TRIGGADALE 1-3
MURDA WAS THE CASE 1-3
By **Elijah R. Freeman**

SLAUGHTER GANG 1-3
RUTHLESS HEART 1-3
By **Willie Slaughter**

GOD BLESS THE TRAPPERS 1-3
THESE SCANDALOUS STREETS 1-3
FEAR MY GANGSTA 1-5
THESE STREETS DON'T LOVE NOBODY 1-2
BURY ME A G 1-5
A GANGSTA'S EMPIRE 1-4
THE DOPEMAN'S BODYGAURD 1&2
THE REALEST KILLAZ 1-3
THE LAST OF THE OGS 1-3
By **Tranay Adams**

MARRIED TO A BOSS 1-3
By **Destiny Skai & Chris Green**

KINGZ OF THE GAME 1-7
CRIME BOSS 1-3
By **Playa Ray**

FUK SHYT
By **Blakk Diamond**

DON'T F#CK WITH MY HEART 1&2
By **Linnea**

ADDICTED TO THE DRAMA 1-3
IN THE ARM OF HIS BOSS
By **Jamila**

LOYALTY AIN'T PROMISED 1&2
By **Keith Williams**

YAYO 1-4
A SHOOTER'S AMBITION 1&2
BRED IN THE GAME
By **S. Allen**

TRAP GOD 1-3
RICH $AVAGE 1-3
MONEY IN THE GRAVE 1-3
CARTEL MONEY
By **Martell Troublesome Bolden**

FOREVER GANGSTA 1&2
GLOCKS ON SATIN SHEETS 1&2
By **Adrian Dulan**

THE STREETS MADE ME 1-3
By **Larry D. Wright**

TOE TAGZ 1-4
LEVELS TO THIS SHYT 1&2
IT'S JUST ME AND YOU
By **Ah'Million**

KINGPIN DREAMS 1-3
RAN OFF ON DA PLUG
By **Paper Boi Rari**

CONFESSIONS OF A GANGSTA 1-4
CONFESSIONS OF A JACKBOY 1-3
CONFESSIONS OF A HITMAN
By **Nicholas Lock**

I'M NOTHING WITHOUT HIS LOVE
SINS OF A THUG
TO THE THUG I LOVED BEFORE
A GANGSTA SAVED XMAS
IN A HUSTLER I TRUST
By **Monet Dragun**

QUIET MONEY 1-3
THUG LIFE 1-3
EXTENDED CLIP 1&2
A GANGSTA'S PARADISE
By **Trai'Quan**

CAUGHT UP IN THE LIFE 1-3
THE STREETS NEVER LET GO 1-3
By **Robert Baptiste**

NEW TO THE GAME 1-3
MONEY, MURDER & MEMORIES 1-3
By **Malik D. Rice**

CREAM 2-3
THE STREETS WILL TALK
By **Yolanda Moore**

THE STREETS WILL NEVER CLOSE 1-3
By **K'ajji**

LIFE OF A SAVAGE 1-4
A GANGSTA'S QUR'AN 1-4
MURDA SEASON 1-3
GANGLAND CARTEL 1-3
CHI'RAQ GANGSTAS 1-4
KILLERS ON ELM STREET 1-3
JACK BOYZ N DA BRONX 1-3
A DOPEBOY'S DREAM 1-3
JACK BOYS VS DOPE BOYS 1-3
COKE GIRLZ
COKE BOYS
SOSA GANG 1&2
BRONX SAVAGES
BODYMORE KINGPINS
BLOOD OF A GOON
By **Romell Tukes**

CONCRETE KILLA 1-3
VICIOUS LOYALTY 1-3
By **Kingpen**

THE ULTIMATE SACRIFICE 1-6
KHADIFI
IF YOU CROSS ME ONCE 1-3
ANGEL 1-4
IN THE BLINK OF AN EYE
By **Anthony Fields**

THE LIFE OF A HOOD STAR
By **Ca$h & Rashia Wilson**

NIGHTMARES OF A HUSTLA 1-3
BLOOD AND GAMES 1&2
By **King Dream**

GHOST MOB
By **Stilloan Robinson**

HARD AND RUTHLESS 1&2
MOB TOWN 251
THE BILLIONAIRE BENTLEYS 1-3
REAL G'S MOVE IN SILENCE
By **Von Diesel**

MOB TIES 1-7
SOUL OF A HUSTLER, HEART OF A KILLER 1-3
GORILLAZ IN THE TRENCHES
By **SayNoMore**

BODYMORE MURDERLAND 1-3
THE BIRTH OF A GANGSTER 1-4
By **Delmont Player**

FOR THE LOVE OF A BOSS 1&2
By **C. D. Blue**

KILLA KOUNTY 1-5
By **Khufu**

MOBBED UP 1-4
THE BRICK MAN 1-5
THE COCAINE PRINCESS 1-10
STEPPERS 1-3
SUPER GREMLIN 1-4
By **King Rio**

MONEY GAME 1&2
By **Smoove Dolla**

MONEY HUNGRY DEMONS 2 | TRANAY ADAMS

A GANGSTA'S KARMA 1-4
By **FLAME**

KING OF THE TRENCHES 1-3
By **GHOST & TRANAY ADAMS**

QUEEN OF THE ZOO 1&2
By **Black Migo**

GRIMEY WAYS 1-3
BETRAYAL OF A G
By **Ray Vinci**

XMAS WITH AN ATL SHOOTER
By **Ca$h & Destiny Skai**

KING KILLA 1&2
By **Vincent "Vitto" Holloway**

BETRAYAL OF A THUG 1&2
By **Fre$h**

THE MURDER QUEENS 1-5
By **Michael Gallon**

FOR THE LOVE OF BLOOD 1-4
By **Jamel Mitchell**

HOOD CONSIGLIERE 1&2
NO TIME FOR ERROR
By **Keese**

PROTÉGÉ OF A LEGEND 1&2
LOVE IN THE TRENCHES 1&2
By **Corey Robinson**

THE PLUG'S RUTHLESS DAUGHTER
By **Tony Daniels**

BORN IN THE GRAVE 1-3
CRIME PAYS
By **Self Made Tay**

MOAN IN MY MOUTH
By **XTASY**

TORN BETWEEN A GANGSTER AND A GENTLEMAN
By **J-BLUNT & Miss Kim**

LOYALTY IS EVERYTHING 1-3
CITY OF SMOKE 1&2
By **Molotti**

HERE TODAY GONE TOMORROW 1&2
By **Fly Rock**

WOMEN LIE MEN LIE 1-4
FIFTY SHADES OF SNOW 1-3
STACK BEFORE YOU SPLURGE
GIRLS FALL LIKE DOMINOES
NAÏVE TO THE STREETS
By **ROY MILLIGAN**

PILLOW PRINCESS
By **S. Hawkins**

THE BUTTERFLY MAFIA 1-3
SALUTE MY SAVAGERY 1&2
By **Fumiya Payne**

THE LANE 1&2
By Ken-Ken Spence

THE PUSSY TRAP 1-5
By **Nene Capri**

DIRTY DNA
By **Blaque**

SANCTIFIED AND HORNY
by **XTASY**

BOOKS BY LDP'S CEO, CA$H

TRUST IN NO MAN
TRUST IN NO MAN 2
TRUST IN NO MAN 3
BONDED BY BLOOD
SHORTY GOT A THUG
THUGS CRY
THUGS CRY 2
THUGS CRY 3
TRUST NO BITCH
TRUST NO BITCH 2
TRUST NO BITCH 3
TIL MY CASKET DROPS
RESTRAINING ORDER
RESTRAINING ORDER 2
IN LOVE WITH A CONVICT
LIFE OF A HOOD STAR
XMAS WITH AN ATL SHOOTER

www.ingramcontent.com/pod-product-compliance
Lightning Source LLC
Chambersburg PA
CBHW070522260626
47161CB00004B/1617